Nightmare Attack

He ran his hand down the small of my back, but before he could get any further I unfroze; lifting my hand and smacking his smooth, hairless face. The sky turned black. The things behind me squealed with what sounded like glee. Kracious grinned.

"All right, you little tease. Have it your way. You want it rough? I've never been one to deny a lady."

I trembled. I knew what was coming. I didn't beg, I just took a step back and balled my hands into fists.

I wanted to know what they were, but I didn't ask. I wouldn't show him my terror. This was a power struggle, and I didn't dare show weakness.

Behind me, the squealing turned to overexcited whistles and pants. Something latched onto my calf; its teeth sinking in with minimal effort on its part, I supposed. I felt them slice through my flesh as if it were hot butter. The skin pulled away.

But I never looked down.

I squeezed my eyes shut. I didn't want to see the nightmares that proceeded to eat me alive – even as I screamed.

The Veil

by Selina Fugate

Nikita,

Hope you enjoy the read!

Selina Fugate ♡

a BlackWyrm book
Louisville, Kentucky

A BlackWyrm Book
BlackWyrm Publishing
10307 Chimney Ridge Ct, Louisville, KY 40299

Printed in the United States of America.

ISBN: 978-1-61318-108-9
LCCN: 2011931868

Edited by Sam Neace, Paul Lewis
Cover design by Dave Mattingly

First edition: July 2011

ACKNOWLEDGMENTS

There are a few people I'd like to thank for making it possible for me to share my writing with others. Mom: God knows that without you kicking my butt the entire way, I would have eventually plopped down and let my love of writing pass me by. Your awesome suggestions are much appreciated, and your faith in me has been my biggest inspiration. I love ya. Mike: thanks for spreading the word and letting me lean on you. You're the best friend a girl could ever have, boog. A big thanks to Bub, Jack, and to my family and friends for your endless source of encouragement. To those that slaved with editing (one werewolf in particular), you're awesome! Dave: thanks for giving me a chance. And to whoever happens to be reading this – your support is very much appreciated!

For Jayden and Cherish
You are my life.
You are my joy.
Mommy loves you.

PROLOGUE

I was seventeen years old when it all began, and seventeen when it ended. Well... life has never been the same, but at least I don't exist in a constant state of paranoia and terror these days. Maybe pieces of my life have been stolen, or altered. It really doesn't matter, because during a particularly miserable fall, for a while, nothing changed. My hair behaved the same exact way; a slight cowlick greeting me in the mirror. I knew what the weather would be, what would be on the radio, and that the neighbors dog would leave a pile of poo rudely on our driveway directly beside of one crumbling brown leaf. That particular maple leaf would tremble in the faint breeze, but was forced to sit beside of that monumental pile of crap due to being stuck on a sharp little crevice in the pavement. Sometimes when I think about it, after the trembling stops, I laugh, because some of that terror was spawned from having to take a particular biology test more than once during the time warp.

You see, during that time, the devil had his hand on the remote control of my life. And if you'll read on, I'll try my best to explain. It's very likely that no one will believe me, but I had to write it down. Why the need to relive the horrors and purge them onto paper? I can't really answer that. I just know that my story has been twisting inside of me; festering, growing, whispering things that I'd rather not remember... The story wants out. If I don't put this on paper, I'm afraid that I'll "project" like any good shrink would say. And trust me, I already have enough crap to deal with and would rather not become totally, irrevocably bonkers. So, let's get the ball rolling, shall we?

CHAPTER 1

Rise and Shine

I woke up at precisely 7:30, late, as usual. I pushed myself up and labored my way out of my queen sized mattress. The bed was my mother's leftovers, but hey, sure as heck beats a single. I could hear my mom's slippered feet padding quickly up the stairs. I rolled my eyes, biting my lip to prevent myself from mockingly reciting the speech which was about to come. I had the gist of it, but somehow she always made it different. So had I recited it, she would have only proved me wrong by saying something else entirely. Yes, that's my mother – always one step ahead of her spawn.

I glanced around my room, batting my lids against the fog and forcing the sleep clogged pipes in my brain to let what I saw trickle through. My room was small, messy, and random, just like me. Pink was the theme, which is odd, because I'm not a big fan of pink. But I had allowed my mother to decorate because she takes such pleasure in shopping. Shopping is something I passionately detest – unless it's for shoes – that is. The only poster on my candy cotton pink walls was of a kitten with his head poking from a box of Kleenex. I didn't remember where I'd gotten it, but I'd never had the heart to take it down. The rest was a clutter of science fiction books and clothing so deep in the floor I was often forced to wade. Beauty magazines were among the litter, but only a few. I made a mental note to clean it when I returned from school. On my bedside perched on a small blond wooden chest of drawers with my black fuzzy lamp, which clashed with the theme and drew the eye. It was my favorite thing in my room. I had just thrown the pink comforter from my body and rose like a disgruntled mummy from her tomb, when she burst through the door in a flurry of flannel shirt and pink fuzzy slippers; her pretty shock of red hair curling at her shoulders.

"Grace! You're not gonna have time for breakfast. Oh God, are you just now getting up? You have that biology test today, right? I'm gonna have to drive you, aren't I? Oh, never mind, never mind, it's all right. I need to grab some milk anyway, but then I'll have to get decent. I mean, I know the grocer won't appreciate my hairy legs and my Betty Boop roos. But then again, maybe he would. That would be even worse."

I stifled laughter. She was genuinely distressed, but even in her anger, she always made me laugh, which could easily become an epic mistake on my part. Laughter in the face of my adorably petite mother's rage was not appreciated, which would result in more anger, and even more laughter on my part, and then, eventually; a grounding. And by *grounded,* I mean I stay at home for a few hours under my mothers pretend glare of disappointment, which eventually dissolves into hugs and a shoo fly release from my comfortable prison. Her heart isn't into hardcore grounding.

She doesn't let me off easy all the time. But I'm generally a good kid. I made good grades, and I'd only been in one fight in fifth grade with Peggy the Predator – the name suited her with her uncanny ability to spot me anywhere and torment me. Thank God she wasn't born with laser beams somewhere on her person. Anyway, back to my point, I never made out with other girls and didn't show my boobs to boys under the bleachers at football games. I had made it to my senior year and it was so far, so good.

I assured her that I would get ready quicker than a roadrunner on speed and she left the room, softly talking to herself the entire way down the stairs. At thirty-nine and the owner of an almost thriving dog grooming business; Jane Sprinter is ultimately my hero. She has an uncanny beauty (which I inherited, somewhat, well, *whatever*, I can dream), that has left more than one man gibbering like a village idiot. 5'5 and Fae petite with a mane of shoulder length red hair that frames a face that's very accurately "peaches and cream," my mom is like a cross between a Victoria's Secret model and a blunt speaking Betty Crocker. She'd somehow gotten blessed with violet eyes (yes, violet), with lashes so dark they look unreal. I remember pulling at them as a child to see if they would come off with a *riiiip*, convinced they were held in place by some type of magical invisible glue. I learned very quickly when she jumped and split her leg on the coffee table, resulting in a shallow cut, that they were, indeed, legit. She was simply stunning, and age only intensified the effect. You see, I've never met my dad.

At twenty-two my mom met Gordon Esmett, a dashing hunk of a douche-bag that courted her for three months, knocked her up, then hit the road. I do sometimes wonder if I resemble him, and from what I've seen of the faded wallet sized photo booth picture they once laughingly took together, I don't look like him in the slightest. He was all smoky darkness while my mother was all fire. His legacy – the unsettling blue of his eyes – was all he'd ever given me. I've sometimes imagined him knocking on the door, and upon my answering saying something like "Who's ya daddy!?" He just seems like that type of flamboyant Rico Sauvé wannabe; though my mother insists he wasn't. *Um, he was in an Elvis cover band for Christ sake.*

Upon her hasty departure of my room I hobbled to the bathroom and sleepily showered and mechanically prepared for the day. School at Birchhound High progressed at a snails pace, with Amy chattering in my ear about her iPhone and its oh-so-frustrating glitches whenever we had lunch. I was pretty confident about my biology test, which was a rarity. Biology was *not* my strong point. And any type of math? Eww. But anything that involves reading I usually thrive at. Literature is my comfort zone. And, though I hate to admit it, I'm pretty damn super in the drama field too. I *love* acting. I find that I can adapt to my characters easily. Anyone will tell you I'm somewhat of a dork but that I tear it up when it comes to Shakespeare. I also *lurve* anything to do with unicorns – however tragic that seems – and my locker is decorated with dozens of stickers of the horned beauties.

I noticed my ex glaring at me from across the room. Adam Bradshaw; jock hunk with female mood swings. "What?" I mouthed, meeting his eyes, even though Amy still loudly ranted her digital woes to me in a stream that she seemed powerless to control. How could the girl talk so long and not turn Smurf blue? God only knows.

Adam simply shook his head and pointedly turned around, waving at an overly painted Erika that always made a point to wear hipster jeans that rode down far enough to reveal her gross sparkly thongs at least once a week. *Ugh. What a ho-cake.* She smiled and shook her junk (and when I say junk, I mean, totally overused junk that isn't fit for human use), as she walked with her tray to the table avoided by girls that didn't have at least four *boy toys* at any given time.

You see, barely a week before that fateful day, I had arrived at Adam's house to study after begging my mother for days to allow it. I assured her his parents would be present, and that the only biology we would be studying would not be the biology of our bodies, but the biology in our textbook. I mean, really, if I really wanted to get all deflowered and stuff, wouldn't I have already done it in the bed of that ugly red Dodge truck of his? I assured her that my virtue wouldn't be put at risk. This earned me one of her surprisingly chilling glares that tend to make me feel 4 years old, and then finally, permission that sounded more like a tired sigh.

Adam had invited me earlier that day in homeroom for the gazillionth time since we'd been dating for a surprisingly romantic six months. Adam hadn't thought I'd be able to actually come. He had assumed my mother would turn me down as usual. It had really put him in a pickle when I'd forgotten to call and showed up on his doorstep; which was answered by Adam and a lipstick smeared Erica that nervously flitted around behind his back like the world's sluttiest butterfly.

Her bleached blond hair had been half falling down from her red ribbon pony tail on one side, and her shirt appeared to be inside out. Adam's parents were certainly *not* present. And unless Erica had suddenly been stricken with an epileptic seizure in Adam's front yard after breaking down and hitching here from her house which was about 10 miles from his residence; they had definitely been doing some up close biology. The look on his face when he saw the look on *my* face could have made someone millions if placed on one of those humorous greeting cards. And in his brilliance – with about as much class as a drunk homeless man doing the Cha-Cha – his only response had been, "I thought you were Josh."

Adam was obviously still sore over our breakup. *Good for him*, I thought with a small smile of satisfaction, which Amy didn't even question as she held up the screen to that blasted iPhone and showed me how the background was stuck on some lame bands image. I didn't really care. I was lost in memories.

CHAPTER 2

Pucker Up

At 3:30 I was home and immediately changing into some sweat pants and my vintage Beatles tee. Jeans, in the house? Not a chance. I'm all for comfort. Oddly – to this day – I remember catching a glimpse of myself in the mirror and touching my face. The heart shaped face staring back at me was obviously about 89% my mothers. The only difference was the paleness of my frosty retinas. A gift (or annoying reminder), from good ol' daddy. It wasn't a stunning face, but it was a good face. I do have to admit in being blessed in the rack department with much thanks to my Mom. I'd also inherited my mother's small frame. My hair was longer than my mother's waves, teasing the small of my back. I toyed with the idea of chopping it off on a regular basis. I imagined myself with a small pair of scissors in each hand; snipping as quickly as the black leather clad Edward, revealing the shape of a giraffe in the hedges of my follicles. But then I would never get a date and would, therefore, never make Adam jealous. It could be suffocating in the summer, but lucky for me and my rats nest, it was mid fall with the barest whisper of winter in the air.

I glanced down at my wrists; at the near frailty of them, the alabaster whiteness of them, and found myself focused on the blue veins there. An odd feeling came over me; a feeling of vulnerability that I wasn't used to; an irrational spike of fear that had no origin. I shook it off. *Probably didn't get enough sleep*, I thought. I had stayed up studying long into the night. Mom was still working and wouldn't clock out until five, so I figured I'd relax as a reward for my success with the biology test. That day, I'd had a bit of awesomeness in my step.

That was how it began.

Walking into the living room I barely took in my surroundings. Our house was a small two story cedar sided den of cozy. Most of the furniture was antique. Not that overly expensive antique stuff, but the old crappy stuff that my mom, sandpaper in hand, had a flair for restoring and making beautiful, Every room was painted white, aside from my pink chaos above. We didn't have a big screen TV, a 30 inch sufficed just fine, even without the coveted flat screen. We rarely watched television. It was all reality TV crap so when my friends were excitedly talking about some new scandal on *Laguna Beach* I was always completely lost, therefore, silent. The only disturbing thing about the house was the dozens of framed photographs of me from infancy until my senior year that covered the walls. Ugh. Too much me-ness.

I plopped down on the floral patterned couch and began the never ending search for our remote. I didn't even have time to celebrate my victorious find which was snugly wedged in between the cushions before the screaming began. I was on my feet and running with total disregard to the furniture around me that begged to crack and bruise my knees. I didn't bother with shoes. Socks would have to suffice. A child, a child, it had to be! I burst out of the front door into the cool breeze, searching my surroundings for the source of the terrible wailing. Birchhound Tennessee was the very definition of slow living, there were rarely screams here, which suited me just fine. The mountains were so high in some spots that they never lost their puffy halo of fog. The weather was often unpredictable, which caused me much conflict with my humid sensitive mane, but I loved it here. I loved the smells, I loved the deer that sometime came into our backyard at night, nervously munching on the fall apples scattered on the ground from that ancient tree I'd climbed so many times as a child. I wasn't a tree hugger, by any means. But I did feel the urge to jump around in the leaves at random times like a third grader.

I liked knowing all of my neighbors by name, although "Formica lane" didn't boast too many of them. We had two families close by, the Dotson's and the Halls. Both had small children. I spotted Ashley, the Hall's 8 year old daughter, kneeling on the one lane road in front of something white and furry. It was interesting when two cars were traveling in different directions, because the width of the road would force one into someone else's driveway until the other passed. The road was quiet, not a car in sight, but the damage was already done. "Oh no," I said aloud, immediately wondering where her parents were, wondering if they knew she was outside by herself.

I rushed to Ashley's side, moving her to the sidewalk even as she reached for the white bundle curled pitifully on the pavement. I tried not to look. Time to focus on Ashley. And move her out of the road. People rarely drove on Formica, but it was no place for an 8 year old. "Where are your parents?" I asked a little more demanding than I should have. And immediately I regretted my harsh tone. Her blond pigtails bounced as she sniffled, and the tears dripped freely onto her blue *Hello Kitty* shirt. "Daddy is in the shower and mommy is at work. He told me to stay in... but... I looked out of the window – and – and... I saw Snowball get hit by a car."

I winced and nervously patted her small back as I told her to stay put, intent on checking out the damage then returning the badly shaken child to her father. I knelt beside of Snowball on the road, grimacing at what I saw. The Persian's white fur was quickly getting gummy with blood. The head – Oh God – the head was practically crushed. No breathing, just the twisted shell of her beloved pet. I lowered my head, fighting nausea. How many times had I watched Ashley playing happily with Snowball? I remembered once how she'd dressed it in a pink dress she'd robbed from one of her dolls and how pissed the feline had looked as she paraded him around from across the street in front of their modest gray one story home.

"GRAAACE!"

Ashley was screaming, and I registered a different kind of fear in her voice, but all too late. I also registered the loud growl of an engine, working far too hard, the frame it powered moving way too fast. I looked up, my eyes wide, and everything sort of went in slow motion. I didn't recognize the man, but I could see his mouth forming a huge O of surprise beneath his brown moustache. I didn't have time to move. The black Ford truck didn't even have the courtesy to break. And ironically, the only thought that passed through was, "Wonder why he's in such a hurry?" before it hit me.

Bones were breaking, snapping, cracking – such sickening sounds and sensations. There wasn't any pain at first. I could feel one tire barrel over my chest, and then another. The air left in a whoosh, leaving me no oxygen to scream with, and somehow that was the worst part. Then my view of the underside of the truck was suddenly replaced with weak, pleasant sunshine, preparing to give way to the darkness of night in the next couple of hours.

Then the pain. The pain. The pain. How could I ever put it into words? *Make it stop. Make it stop. MAKE IT STOP*, my brain chanted to the atmosphere, to the pavement, to the child screaming beside of me, to the universe. But it didn't. I floated in and out of blackness, welcoming it, embracing it, but fighting it to the best of my ability and praying for it to recede. *I'm dying*, I thought. *I'm dying.* Strange thoughts assaulted me. Trivial things; I'd never get to savor that A on my biology test. I'd never again feel Amy's skilled fingers, running through my hair, fussing over its unruly style in the girl's bathroom, trying to make me her version of presentable. I'd never again feel my mother's arms around me, breathe in her scent, which was usually some type of apple scented dog shampoo which I both teased her about and adored. I'd never taste those homemade chocolate bars she was so good at making. Oh no... mom... mom... *my mommy*. I was sorry. I tried to send to her my apology, with something that was half prayer and half desperate attempt at telepathy. How would she cope?

I thought I was crying, I felt wetness on my face, but some morbid part of me knew instinctively that it wasn't tears. People were standing over me. Ashley's dad, Bill. Miranda Dotson – the pretty 20-something whom had just celebrated the birth of her son with her husband and close family not even three days ago in their flat brick ranch style home. Their screaming sounded like a chorus in hell. There was so much shouting, people, and then more people. My breathing was wet. Not enough air. No air. And the pain it took to draw it in, it couldn't be tolerated. I knew I couldn't make the effort any longer. Something was wrong in my chest – something deflated – a burst balloon. Something was grinding, gritty, when I exhaled. Sharp things wiggled their way up inside of my throat, tearing it. I threw a small prayer out to God. I'd never really went to church, but in that moment, I hoped that if I were worthy of Heaven, that God would take me in. Maybe Snowball would be there too. After all, if Disney was right, and dog's go to heaven, then why can't cats?

And then something even more bizarre happened. Some hallucination, no doubt, before I passed to whatever awaited me on the other side. There was a man. And the pain, well, the pain stopped and the people around me paused in mid sob. The soft breeze seemed to stop blowing, becoming as thick as syrup, holding everything in place, in animated suspension.

The man, *wow*, he was beautiful. His smile was bright, seeming on the verge of giddy laughter. *What a perfect frickin' nose,* my poor dying brain mused in its delirium. How old was he? 18? 29? 39? He had no age; I guess perfection doesn't have one. And back to that nose, it was very bold, roman deliciousness, if a nose can be called delicious. His raven black hair hung around my face as he knelt on the ground above my head, looking down at me. It was soft, like he'd used the conditioner of the God's and blow dried it with the angels' hairdryer. Angels – that had to be it. Yes, he was an angel – an angel had come to guide me to the other side! And what a beautiful angel he was! *But wait* – I thought – *his eyes, they're all wrong.* Something was very wrong. Even though I was viewing his features from upside down as he knelt there, I registered that something was missing, something that should be there in an angelic being. His eyes weren't of any color of the rainbows I used to search for desperately during sunny rains as a child. There were no whites, no pupil, just, blackness. Like two expertly carved black stones from the creek out back, they bore into me, shiny, glazed, and terrible.

My expression must have changed from awe to horror because he threw back that beautiful mane of hair and laughed at the sky. *What's happening? Who is he? Am I not going to Heaven? Am I going somewhere else?* I panicked. I tried to move, to thrash, to run, but I was immobilized. Dead, *Oh God I'm dead,* I thought. *The pain is gone and I'm dead* – my mind screamed – because my voice couldn't. *I am going to Hell – and I won't even have the pleasure of screaming as I descend.* But had I really been that bad? Had I really been so unworthy? I'd stolen a pack of gum when I was ten when mom was low on cash during her early struggles with her business. But other than that, had I broken so many of the commandments? I tried desperately to remember what they were. I tried to make sense of the damning, but I couldn't. I could only scream in my head and pray that this was all a nightmare.

"Relax," he said, and he knelt over me once more. The smile was still there, but his full lips covered the perfect whiteness of his teeth. "I'm not the devil. I know what you're thinking. I'm not that cool – just almost."

He stifled a small laugh. His voice was like velvet, the type of voice that could be belted from a microphone and make women throw their bra's on the stage, praying like hell that he'd grab one and take it backstage with him, therefore, taking an intimate piece of her with him as well. But there was meanness there too in the casual shifting of his weight from foot to foot, in the twitching of his mouth as he struggled not to laugh as I lay there broken.

He reached down and stroked my cheek, and that I could feel through the numbness. His touch was like fire – fire and sex (or what I imagined sex would be like), and cool watery silk all at once. He spoke, "I am here to make a proposition. Sometimes I spot someone, and I just can't help myself. I want to play. Do you like to play, Grace?"

The confusion whirled. *What the hell? Someone help me!* I begged to the everything. *Where's everyone? Where are Ashley, Miranda, and Bill? Why weren't they helping me?* I pulled my eyes away from his magnetism long enough to glimpse those around me, and was further horrified. They weren't moving. There were paused. Ashley's head rested on her father's shoulder as she clung to him and he packed her away. He was frozen in mid stride, looking back, the look on his face one of pity and horror.

"I'll take that as a yes," he laughed silkily, "Anyway, again, I am here to make a proposition. I've been watching you, Grace, and even though you're a bit boring, I *know* there's something special inside of you. Not to mention, you're quite fetching, and *female*. *Men* are no fun. They're not half as pleasing to the eye. You're mature for your age, and, being a man of good taste, I like that. And oh, you're ever so pretty. If I were the type of man to settle down, I'd come callin' on you in my Sunday's best. But here's the deal, *Sweet Cheeks*. You're dying. You're splattered all over the pavement like little Snowball over there." He cocked his head towards the direction of my feet. *If I still have feet*, the morbid voice in my brain countered.

"And if you want to live," he continued, "I can allow it. I can fix you because – oh dear," he paused dramatically. "What will your mother do when she comes home from scrubbing K-9's all day to find that her golden girl was just crushed beneath the pickup truck of a drunk driver? Not to mention, he'll get away with it, just a fun little fact!" He laughed again and I longed to sob, to scream. There was an anger bubbling inside of me too. He'd mentioned my mom. Oh God, was he going to go after my mom?

Terror made my eyes roll back in my head, and although I couldn't feel them, his cheerful face was replaced by blackness with brief flashes of light. I thought of my mother meeting a fate like my own, and it was too horrible to even contemplate. Even in death, my temper flared. I tried to convey my anger with my expression, if my face was able to do such a thing, and suddenly his laughing was in overdrive.

"Those ginger girls sure do carry some fire," he teased. "You're a lot like her, you know? Fascinating woman, she is, but you're just a little more amusing in your youth. You have more energy, more, *pizzazz*." My eyes rolled back into focus; taking in my tormentor and trying to memorize his face. I was dying, I knew, but if the afterlife allowed me to haunt the earth, then I'd find him and be one hell of an annoying spook. He bent even closer, his hair falling over my brow, fine strands snaking into my eyes, obscuring my weakening vision.

He never took his eyes from mine as he talked, "Think about it, Grace, do you really want her to see you like this? She's due home anytime now, you know. Not to mention little Ashley is going to be traumatized for life if you croak right here in front of her house. Already she loses Snowball and then sees her neighbor go *splat*. And you're so young. You have so much to do... so many experiences that you haven't had yet." He raised a little, his hair no longer in my eyes. He stuck his lower lip out and pouted, wiping at imaginary tears. Then he brightened, his body seeming to crackle with energy.

He rushed on, "Even better, what if I could make you 17 forever? You'd never age. And you'd be alive. Ah, just imagine! You'd be alive and well and still able to hug your mom when she comes through the door. And oh, by the way, darling, your arms are broken in more places than even *I* could count. Your ribs are all shattered, your lungs, deflated full of blood, nonetheless, and if you could only see how much blood is coming from your mouth and ears, you wouldn't find that pleasing at all. No, no, not a bit." He stopped.

Who was he? What was he talking about?

He seemed to be losing patience when he said, "Two more minutes, Grace. Two more before you're dead forever. Two minutes before your mother is burying you in the ground and the worms have their claim. Mere seconds before everyone you know is sobbing and saying, 'Poor Grace, she died so young.' And poor Amy, you're her best friend, you know? Even though she emits a type of shallowness I find irritating, she loves you dearly. So choose, choose now, time is running out." He bent over me, and though I couldn't feel my body, I could feel his breath on my lips.

He sounded so convincing, "So kiss me, Grace, kiss me and seal the deal. I'm a phenomenal kisser, by the way. Trust me, you'll never experience another smackaroo quite like it!" The strange vision coaxed. This inspired another fit of giggling from him, and made me long to sucker punch him. But at the same time, was it true? Could I live and be seventeen forever? Could it really be that bad? Oh, to spare my mother, to spare everyone, to breathe air into my lungs. Oh God, could it really be? Was he really some type of angel with a twisted sense of humor, or the devil after all? I wanted to graduate – I wanted to go to college – I wanted to marry and have kids and laugh and cry and grow old and be filled with memories of a full life.

I didn't think, couldn't think, and time was running out. Blackness was filling my vision, I was dying. It was the end. I didn't take the time to marvel as what I somehow knew to be my spirit began twitching and pushing it's way out, floating, maybe even evaporating.

"Yes," I tried to breathe. "Yes, do it. Kiss me." But I couldn't speak. Nothing came, not even exhalations. My eyes drifted closed, but my expression must have given consent. I was vaguely aware that the sky grew a little darker as he slowly pressed his perfect lips to mine.

He was right; it was unlike anything I had experienced. The world exploded in light, and I was swirling through the universe at high speed. I saw colors that were so alien they couldn't have a name. Scenes from my childhood flitted by like a movie on rewind. My birthday parties, my mother wiping icing from my mouth after I'd put my face in a plate of cake at 2. I fast forwarded through the time I'd broken my toe on that hidden rock in my Granny's backyard. My mother and I dancing in the living room with Elmo on Sesame Street, what I was, what I wasn't, and what I could have been. And now, looking back, had

I really thought it all through, I would have realized that nothing is free. There's always some catch, isn't there? And can I say for sure that I would have still kissed him and sealed my fate? No. I don't think I would have. The cost was far too high.

CHAPTER 3

Been There – Done That

I awoke at precisely 7:30 AM from what had to have been a terrible nightmare. A sob tore from my throat as I sat straight up in bed, clutching the pink comforter to my chest. It was just a nightmare. Oh God, *it was only a nightmare.* I breathed in deeply without any pain, I ran my hands over my legs, my arms, my face, which I cradled in my shaking hands and sobbed into with the sweetest relief I'd ever felt. It was Thursday, because yesterday I had taken the biology test... wait... I sniffled and wiped at my nose with the back of my hand like an unsanitary child, careless of the snot that was no doubt covering it now. Yesterday... yesterday... the last thing before I visited what could have only been the darkest corner of my imagination, what was I doing? Sitting on the couch? But what about after that, and when did mom come home? Did I fall asleep there in the living room? Did mom somehow carry me like a burly mountain man UP to my room? I was far from porky but at hundred and eight pounds, impossible for my mother to carry that far, she being a whopping hundred and twenty-eight pounds herself. Impossible, unless I sleep walked here. And that would mean that I had been asleep for a total of – I looked at the clock – fourteen hours! What the hell?

I gingerly threw the comforter back and cautiously put my feet on the floor, slowly standing with my forehead scrunched up. I shook my head hard, trying to clear the fog. Perhaps the trauma of the nightmare had affected me more than I'd thought. I looked towards the door as I heard the familiar sound of my mother padding up the stairs. 7:30. I was late for school. She opened the door and walked in, wearing a flannel gown, and pink fuzzy slippers. Not unusual – perhaps she was just wearing the same thing she'd worse yesterday. But the surreal oddness that came in the form of words from her pretty mouth made me go weak in the knees.

"Grace! You're not gonna have time for breakfast. Oh God, are you just now getting up? You have that biology test today, right? I'm gonna have to drive you, aren't I? Oh, never mind, never mind, it's all right. I need to grab some milk anyway, but then I'll have to get decent. I mean, I know the grocer won't appreciate my hairy legs and my Betty Boop roos. But then again, maybe he would. That would be even worse."

Betty Boop roos? She'd worn those yesterday. This had to be the most powerful déjà-vu ever. "Mom," I managed, swallowing hard. "Didn't you wear that gown, and those undies, yesterday morning?" She looked at me as if I were on an acid trip and hittin' the sauce at the same time.

"What, Grace? No, not that I recall. I haven't been wearing the same underwear for 2 mornings straight." She laughed, making light of my question, but I could see the concern in those vivid violet eyes. I could see her calculating, running through reasons, explanations.

"But what about the biology test. I took that yesterday, and... I did great."

"What?" She asked, looking genuinely confused.

"My test," I began.

She cut me off. "I think I would have known yesterday if you'd taken it, especially if you did a great job on it. You wouldn't pass up the bragging rights. You never mentioned that to me. You told me last night that it would be today."

"Honey," she said as she crossed the distance between us until she was standing right in front of me. "Are you not feeling well? Here," she pressed the back of her cool hand to my forehead, and softly repeated the same move with my cheeks. "You look like you've seen a ghost."

It was only when I'd dropped my head to let her feel my forehead that I realized what I was wearing. I was clad in the same white tee, the same blue pajama bottoms, and the same *Mickey Mouse* socks. (Shut up, I know what you're thinking, but they're for in-room use, only). The Déjà-vu hit me again like a drug, blocking out all thought and all sensation for a split second. I staggered a bit, grabbing my mothers forearm for balance and slowly looked up into her face. "I'm fine, mom. Big biology test... you know. I stayed up late studying."

I left her standing in confusion and went into the bathroom that connected to my room and cleaned up as quickly as possible. I ended up lingering in front of the mirror a little longer than necessary, looking at my reflection, wondering if I really was sick. In a state of numbness I made my way downstairs, left with my mother and stared blankly from the car window all the way to Birchhound High. I felt like blowing chunks when I saw the Birchhound community banks digital clock blinking its red numbers that blared brightly in the weak morning light. It read, "Wednesday, 17th, 8:05 AM."

In third period I squinted at the test, tapping the eraser of my lead pencil on the scratched surface of my single, suddenly unbearably uncomfortable desk. I knew this stuff, but it was almost like trying to catch a single floating seed from a dandelion in a windstorm. It was there, all right, but out of my reach; swirling and drifting higher and higher just when I was ready to capture it in my hands. The weird déjà-vu kept blasting me, until I felt as if I were predicting every occurrence. Tyler getting up to sharpen his pencil loudly, earning the glares of students tying to concentrate. The chubby kid – Sam Whicker – sat directly to my right, that looking as if he'd been wedged into the desk. He'd broke wind and was looking sheepishly around, praying no one had heard it. But boy, *did I smell it.*

This had all happened before, I thought, *and now Tabitha Hanley's cell phone will ring, and Mrs. Stacy will confiscate it.* I almost choked on my own saliva when, indeed, it happened. My look of horror outshined Tabitha's at having her lifeline stolen. Mrs. Stacy peered oddly at me, and I quickly looked back down at my test. *Eenie... meanie... miny... moe...*

I knew what would happen as I walked into the lunchroom. Amy would rant about her iPhone, Adam would glare at me, then turn his attentions to Ericka, who would strut by like the stank hooker she was. But when it played through, I stood up, leaving Amy's mouth agape. Without an explanation, I escaped to the nurse's station, leaving my lunch – gross looking spaghetti and partially burned garlic loaf – all but untouched.

Birchhound high wasn't a very large school, boasting only about 500 students, so the majority of students were pretty much on a first name basis with the staff. Mrs. Sharon – the school nurse – repeated my mother's investigation of my forehead and cheeks. "You don't feel feverish, Grace, what're your symptoms?"

What to say? I wondered. I imagined something like, "*Mrs. Sharon, I suddenly woke up this morning to what seems to be yesterday and discovered that I could predict every occurrence since then. You know, like a psychic. You see, last night I had a dream that I died, and the Devil all but made out with me. I'm thinking it's all maybe the result of an alien abduction, or perhaps I'm one of those weird indigo children that I've seen on Oprah. Or maybe I'm just batshit?*" But instead I said, "Oh... my stomach is upset. My mom and I stopped at the diner for breakfast and I think the hash browns were funk." She frowned a little, as if scenting out my crappy lie and led me back to the sickroom to lie down on the small white cot. She told me to rest, and insisted that if I didn't feel better within the next 20 minutes to ask the front office to phone my mother and arrange for pickup.

I lay down and sighed as she turned off the light. Light shone in from her station but she had the courtesy to close to door, leaving it only cracked. Now... I thought... now I could cry. Now I could partially acknowledge the fact that I was currently losing my mind. As the school stoners would say, I was 'trippin' balls,' but without the help of a stimulant. What was happening to me?

I cowered on the cot, embracing the fact that I didn't know what would happen in the nurses station outside, that I couldn't predict when she would shoo me out to the front office, or back to class. I had to be sick. I *had* to be delirious, but without the fever that usually accompanies that. Some type of exotic flu or maybe – and the thought chilled me to the bone – *something growing in my brain*. Maybe I was a victim of some hard disgusting kernel, nurtured and grown by my own hypocritical body, pushing at the delicate tissue and scrambling my thoughts. A brain tumor... could it be?

Dr. Stanley, our family physician – a smart man with an all too obvious crush on my mother – yes, he was the answer. My mother could take me to see Dr. Stanley first thing in the morning. Since I'd been little, I'd been solid in my conviction that Dr. Stanley could fix anything. He'd probably say it was some weird side effect from some weird overload of (eww) teenaged hormones. Or he'd tell me that it was some exotic Japanese flu that caused paranoia and hallucinations. Or he could inform us, sadly, with a tremble of his bearded chin and a sad tearful sparkle in his warm eyes, that it was a brain tumor.

And as if to confirm my paranoia, a voice, a silky, eerily familiar voice, one that I could never forget, whispered from everywhere and nowhere at the same time, "Adam is quite upset with you, you know... so very upset about your breakup." Laughter bounced inside of my skull and I grabbed my head, placing my hands over my ears. What? What did it mean? What did Adam have to do with any of this? My mind was producing random audio hallucinations, yes, that had to be it.

I noticed a shadowy movement above my head and rose slowly, pushing myself up from the cot in what I hoped would cause the least amount of noise. On the wall beside of me something skittered, something tiny. It made a chattering sound, and at first I thought it to be a cricket. Sometimes they squeezed into my house and I'd catch them, following their chirping sound that could drive you nuts if you didn't find them. But as I listened, the chattering changed. It became tiny laughter. Tiny, insectile laughter.

Crazy, crazy, I'm going crazy. Crazy crazy... crazy, I thought.

I sat up on the cot just as Mrs. Sharon walked in, giving a little gasp. "Grace! I had forgotten all about you! And – oh dear – now you've missed your other classes! Why didn't you remind me?"

I was still stunned by the mysterious voice, still reeling with fear, but I managed a lie that slipped out as if on an automatic factory belt, "Sorry... I... I must have fallen asleep."

"Well," she said, "School is out in a short 10 minutes so you'd better start waking up pretty quickly." She turned and walked out, her step conveying her agitation. Her hilariously authentic nurse's uniform swishing as she walked. She thought me to be playing hooky. But why should I care? I had bigger fish to fry. After all, my brain was melting. I made my way to my last period and walked through the door, earning the stares of everyone, including Mr. Prater, my Social Studies instructor.

"Grace," he said, mockingly pleasant, "So nice of you to join us." That earned a few tired giggles from a few students, but I ignored them. I all but stumbled my way to my desk, enveloped in a fog, where the only thing that was clear was the persistent voice of my conscience telling me I was on a one way trip to Crazyville.

Almost everyone was already shoving their notebooks into book bags; or yanking out their blackberries to check for deliciously gossipy text messages, but I barely glanced at them as I moved to my assigned seat in the back. I was looking at Adam, and he was looking right back, and I swear, the expression on his face wasn't just mere anger, it was hate; a look so full of malice that I actually cringed. He'd never looked at me like that before, and to think of it, I'm not sure Adam had ever looked at anyone like that before. He's generally a very nice guy. Sure, he's a macho player wannabe, but he's not hateful. Unlike most jocks, he'd never picked on anyone beneath his school status, one of his redeeming qualities in my eyes. He certainly went against the grain to date me. I mean, not that I felt honored or anything. Geez. But God knows I'm not Miss. Popular; nor do I want to be. I don't like an abundance of attention. I was happy with my current place in my little circle, and, honestly, we weren't that far down on the food chain.

I plopped down into my seat, frowning, and wondering what I'd done to deserve that type of reaction. I met his eyes, his pretty, brown eyes. He was about 6'1 – jet black hair stylishly spiked in the front and messy – although I knew he'd spent at least 30 minutes on it. We sometimes chatted on the phone while he did his hair before leaving for school because we didn't have first period together. He was a senior, too, although he looked more like a hunky college guy. His walk was something to watch and I could tell it was practiced. He was muscular, but not to the point of gross and veiny. He had a ready smile and an infectious, sexy laugh.

I was trying to find something to excuse his current super-douche behavior. But he just stared into my eyes, looking as if he could cross the distance and backhand me right there in my seat. I wrinkled my brow in confusion. What did he have to be mad about? He was the one that had cheated and likely (and hopefully), caught VD from Erika, aka *Whore of Babylon*.

I remembered the strange voice (the voice belonging to the mysterious man in my recent nightmare) telling me that Adam was upset. What did it mean? Yeah, he was upset, he didn't have a chance of getting into my pants after cheating on me with the school whore, but why did that matter? And why did I even care? I was in the process of losing my mind. Reflecting on Adam's past sins would have to wait. But still, something about the odd message the voice had given me sent a shiver up my spine. Not to mention the cackling cricket, or whatever it was. I did not want to muse on what else it could have been. Something was wrong, and Adam was in the middle of it.

I kept looking at Adam for at least a minute, until he lifted his football jacket (number 26) and pulled a gun from the waistband of his expensive Calvin Klein jeans. Immediately thoughts of his possible new STD left my mind. He pointed the shiny hand gun at my head from only two seats over to my right, and cocked it. My eyed widened. Kevin Bailey, who I swear looks just like Harry Potter (and had been dreamily staring at me), saw my stunned expression, turned around to see the cause of my distress, and ducked.

Adam pulled the trigger. I'm sure there were screams, I'm sure there was gore, and panic, but I didn't hear any of these things. I don't even recall hearing the inevitable blast. I didn't even have time to ask myself "Why?" There was only a brief sharp explosion of pain and light, a sickening bliss, and then, nothing.

CHAPTER 4

Let's Play

I was sitting in a plush high backed chair, my hands on the embroidered armrests. The material was velvet, purple velvet. Along the center of the rests, beneath my forearms, ran a strip of wood perhaps 3 inches thick, and upon further inspection, I realized the expertly carved designs in the wood were tiny laughing skeletons. Where was I?

I looked around to my right, blackness, everywhere, blackness. I stared directly in front of me. I was at a table – a circular cherry beauty that looked very expensive and very antique – with the same laughing skeletons carved along the edges. I jumped when I saw him, illuminated by the small stained glass lamp that sat in the table's center, knocking my foot on the sturdy bear clawed leg of the table. The stained glass pocked his beautiful face with flecks of blue, yellow, and red light. He smiled, that carnivorous expression gleaming brighter than any lamp. His empty eyes raked over me rudely, and then returned to meet my own, making my breath catch in my throat.

"Hello... Clairece," he said in a bone chilling imitation of Hannibal. He threw back his mane of silken blackness and laughed. I was noticing his skin, smooth as an infant's, poreless, grotesque perfection. He sat in a chair identical to mine – as far as I could tell – looking like some gothic king.

"Where am I?" I asked, breathless. But then I remembered... the nurse's station... Adam... gunfire... No. "Adam – Adam would never – it couldn't have been real. Where am I?" I asked, panic making my voice climb higher.

He raised a finger to his full lips, "Shh," he said. "I thought you'd be pleased to see me, after our hot kisses there on the blood splattered pavement and all." I shut my eyes, not knowing which would be worse. To have all of this *really* be happening, or be completely bonkers and imagining it all.

As if reading my thoughts, he laughed. "It's all real, you know. And I've never gotten to formally introduce myself. Let's try this again, shall we? I find that I wasn't very polite the last time, why, I didn't even give you a name!"

I glared at him as my breath quickened with fright.

"Hi!" He said in an overly perky businessman-like voice, "I'm Kracious, dark sorcerer extraordinaire. I am so pleased to meet you." He looked at me expectantly, a comical frown on his face, his tone hurt. "How rude, Grace. You know, I think mannerisms peaked during the late 1800's. How I loved watching the ladies curtsy and the gentleman bow at the waist. Somewhat annoying, though, whenever I'd choose a woman during that time, she always fainted when I approached due to those horrid, tight corsets they'd wear. Horrible contraptions! It annoyed me so much that I would usually make her death more painful than necessary, and final. I was more into men anyway, during that time period." He wagged his brows at me and winked conspiratorially.

"Why are you telling me these things? What do you want from me?" I asked.

"Ugh," he said, rolling his eyes. His voice changed then suddenly becoming my own – right down to the frightened tremble. "What do you want from me?" He mocked. "Where am I?" I gasped and he giggled, though with less amusement than before. "Really... how boring. It's always the same questions, and I do tire of repetition. I've lived a very long time, Grace, a very long time. Do you know how boring life can be when you're immortal, just watching hundreds of years sluggishly pass?" He sighed, and a crystal goblet suddenly appeared on the table in front of him out of thin air. He picked it up, swished the bright red liquid inside, and lifted it to his nose. He sniffed it, closing his eyes, savoring whatever aroma wafted to him.

What was that, I wondered on some far away level, the blood of virgins?

He sighed, "I do enjoy a good Merlot while I'm terrorizing innocents."

I stared intently at him, the black of his eyes as they peered at the goblet in his hand. He leaned back, his posture relaxed. I shook my head, trying to form words in my brain to verbalize, but failing miserably. He flicked his wrist, and I jumped. I was suddenly in black and white striped jailbird attire, right down to the little striped hat.

He tossed his hair back, smoothing it from his brow. "Oh, don't look at me like that, Grace, or I'll make you look even worse. If you're going to act like a shell shot prisoner, you may as well look like one." Shackles appeared, chaining my legs and arms together. The weight from the shackles made me involuntarily lean forward. I looked down. There was no floor, I could feel it, but it was as if I were looking into a black abyss. I looked up, and from no specific direction, Elvis started belting "Jail house rock."

"Answer me, please," I managed weakly. "Tell me what you want."

"And it speaks!" He boomed loudly, rising to stand, spreading his arms wide and throwing his head back like a Pentecostal preacher in the heat of a sermon. From somewhere, the sound of an audience's oohs and aahs met my ears; a disembodied crowd, a crowd that didn't exist.

"And about our little deal..." He paced slowly back and forth, those beautiful pianist hands clasped at his back. "I was a bit dishonest with you. You won't live forever. You'll live as long as I see fit. You'll live as long as you amuse me, and lucky for you, I find you very amusing, Grace." He stopped pacing and met my eyes. I stared back, wondering if at any moment I would be sucked into them, sucked into that awful black nothingness that seemed to be his very essence. He radiated sickness, he reeked of cruelty, but he also had an allure, a very strange and horrifying allure that made me want to agree to anything he asked. His voice made me want him not look upon me with amusement, but with affection. *What the f...*

I had just been shot, in the *friggin'* head, and all I could do was stare at this – this... *thing* with a horrible fascination that betrayed everything in my heart and tainted everything innocent in my soul. I reached up to my face, feeling for blood, a sign, anything that would confirm my strong suspicion that the bad thing that had just happened in the class room, really DID happen. But my hand – although shaking visibly – came away dry.

He smiled gently and took on the stance and tone of a patient teacher. "Grace, you're in between realities at the moment. You know, the "astral plane" that only hippies seem to take an interest in now days. But you're dead dear, dead as a doornail, just much prettier. Yes, Adam sent you out of that world with a bullet to the brain, but not without a little subliminal persuasion. I assure you."

He walked towards me – no – he *slinked* towards me, as graceful as a black leopard appreciating it's crippled prey, right before it sinks it's fangs into the softness of it's neck and rips through the pulsating jugular. I instinctively pushed myself against the back of the chair, the shackles forcing my feet from the ground as my hands pulled them along.

He was wearing a leather sleeveless shirt. It seemed to have been patched together in pieces, decoratively, awesomely, with shiny metal wires. His leather pants, made of the same material, clung to his lower body like a glove. His knee high black lace up boots made little *clock* sounds and he slowly made his way towards me. He paused at my side and lifted a lock of my hair, letting it slip through his white smooth fingers. He caught the tips of the lock, and, closing his eyes and sniffing delicately, he seemed to blissfully savor the scent as he had the wine. The words came before I finished the thoughts.

"I'm gonna wake up again, aren't I? I'm gonna wake up, it's gonna be Wednesday, and I'm going to die."

I said this, and almost cringed, as if just uttering the words made what I was saying more real, more terrible. That changed me in a way that would alter me forever, even though I find it impossible to fully put into words. It was a conviction, a numb acceptance. I was willing to die. I was shakily accepting my fate. I had tasted death too much already. Once was enough; twice, the breaking point. This was a daily death sentence I was powerless to escape, never knowing how it would happen. Never knowing exactly when it would happen. I didn't want it. I wanted to die, to sleep, but not to wake up anymore. But then again... Just thinking of the people I would leave behind... the dreams I would forfeit, I doubted my conviction. But wouldn't my dreams be demolished anyway? How can anyone accomplish anything of any meaning if you're curled up with the grim reaper the entire time, his breath, tickling every thought, reminding me.

Kracious raised one slender boned long hand and placed the back of it on his forehead. He used the other to fan his face, his mouth opening in a mocking *O* of horror. He sniffled and tossed his hair in a perfect feminine impersonation. I hated him.

"Let me stay dead," I spoke again, feeling as if someone else had taken over my body – a more rational Grace – who said what the terrified Grace would never be able to say. Why live just to die, over and over again? Such an adult decision, I thought. Shouldn't that be what I wanted with all of my heart? But it wasn't. It was, and it wasn't at the very same time.

In a blur he had my prison cap in his hands. He held it directly in front of my face, pulling something ridiculously large out of the very small cap. I should have closed my eyes, I shouldn't have stared at the bloody, mangled ball of fur, but I couldn't look away. It was snowball. His crushed head was oozing maggots and pink fluid dripped onto my jailbird pants. Half of his brain was exposed and his back legs twitched, as if dreaming of chasing fat field mice in his backyard. His one good eye – the one that wasn't burst like a fat grape – was looking at me. He seemed to be blaming me. He seemed to mock me. I could almost swear that I saw a flicker of satisfaction in that remaining good eye; something too human to be real. He meowed. I screamed, twisting my head, trying to escape the awful sight, but my eyes refused to close, glued open by horror.

"Tada! I always found rabbit's very cliché. An EXCELLENT party trick, my dear!" He loudly boomed.

He then bent over double with laughter – holding his middle as the mirth shook his body – all the while keeping Snowball suspended before my face. After the outburst, he lowered Snowball back into the tiny cap, and placed it back on my head. I jerked my head and my body seized in panic until it flew off, landing top side up on the blank nothingness beneath us which was somehow solid. I wheezed, tilting my head as I looked inside, dreading what might crawl out next, I saw that, once again, it was only an ordinary, ugly prison cap. I wanted to tear at the horrible attire, the ridiculously flamboyant costume which fit me perfectly, it's long sleeves seemingly tailored to the exact length of my arms. It reminded me of the prison garb wore in "O' brother where art thou?"

I was powerless, at his mercy, but that didn't stop me from turning my head and looking right into those reptilian eyes and spitting. That's right – not a very feminine thing to do – but words alone could not convey my disgust. The spittle missed his face – my original mark – and landed on the front of his awesomely cool shirt. His face took on an expression of disgust as he glanced down.

"How rude! How very rude of you, Grace!" And with a flick of his wrist the spittle was gone – or perhaps a new shirt had appeared – who knows? He sniffed his distaste, "Here I stand, attempting to make polite conversation with you, and this is how I'm repaid? Ungrateful child... tsk... tsk." He inhaled sharply and playfully swatted my thigh.

He flicked his wrist once more and my attire changed, suddenly becoming that of *Alice in Wonderland*. I didn't have to look to know there was a blue ribbon in my hair, which matched the puffy dress. Knee high stockings – white as snow – traveled out of my tiny, black kid slippers. A multicolored sucker the size of my head then materialized in his hand, and he held it out, as if in offering. "I'm afraid now that I'm going to have to withhold this due to what a naughty girl you've been."

"Bastard," I snarled, placing my fear on the back burner. "I don't know what you're trying to do, or what game you're playing, but if you're going to let me live just to die again, then kill me. Kill me now, make it final, make it real!" I gasped, because the voice coming from my throat was not my own, but the cartoonish breathless voice of the animated *Alice*. I wanted to scream. I hated myself for the angry tears that coursed down my cheeks, lest they be mistaken for tears of fear.

"Not a chance, pumpkin," he laughed as I struggled with the shackles, longing to thrash him, to smack and pinch his perfect skin, to tear out his perfect hair. But it was useless.

He did a little jig, and if a jig could be graceful, this was it. A huge smile lit his features and he paused, extended one leg, stretching out his arm, his palm up, as if to offer his hand for a waltz. He then straightened and turned in a circle, his arms extended as he softly sang, "I'm mad, you're mad, we're all mad here!"

He cackled, the sound so loud it seemed to vibrate my teeth. Then he asked, "Why are you so angry, Grace? I'm only giving you what you wanted; the chance to live. Why stop the game so soon after I put so much effort into staking you out? No, no, not a chance. That will simply not do. We're going to play, Grace. I already told you that, but" – He paused. There was no way out. No way out and I knew it. But then – "I like to play fair," he all but purred. "If you can stay alive until midnight, you win, Grace, and I leave you forever. Life for you will pick up where it left off."

It was my one ray of hope, my chance at life, a glimmer of hope.

"Well then," I said, and noticed my voice was my own again. Then a little smile of my own formed – a bitter thing that spoke more than any words could convey. "I'll just have to find a way to beat you, then." My words were brave, yes, but certain, absolutely not. But I had to try. I had to. If this was my cross to bear, then I would fight the weight every step of the way. After all, I had already died, TWICE, what was the worst that could happen? I would likely die again, but it wasn't like death and I were strangers now. Not bosom buddies; but strangers, nope.

"I knew ya had it in ya!" He laughed and bounced in place like an excited, hyper child.

Then he stopped moving, and leaned in towards my face until his lips were mere inches from mine. His breath was warm and smelled, oddly, of peppermint – peppermint, and, what... sulfur? But I didn't recoil, I didn't flinch. I met his black eyes, lifting my chin in defiance.

He practically danced as he leaned even closer and pressed his lips to my ear. "And the butterfly is bursting from her cocoon. This pleases me, Grace. You and I are going to be such good friends. I just know it!" I squeaked embarrassingly as his warm tongue touched the delicate skin behind my ear, then it moved, serpentine, making a trail across my neck and cheek. He paused at my lips, kissed both corners softly, then moved to nibble on my chin. I almost closed my eyes, and before I could remember myself, a little sigh of pleasure escaped my lips. I was tilting my head back, trying to move in my restraints to give him easier access to my body until I heard his soft, mocking laughter. I jerked away, a disgusted growl escaping my throat. He laughed louder.

"Game on!" he shouted in my ear.

CHAPTER 5

Uninvited Guests

I was awaking again at precisely 7:30AM, but this time, with a mission. I threw back the comforter and bolted out of bed, swaying a little and almost tripping over a discarded pair of jeans. I cocked my head and waited, waited for the sound of my mothers slippers on the stairs. I wasn't disappointed. I didn't bother looking myself over, I knew that I was whole, and I knew what I was wearing. My mother burst through the door in her flannel gown, her mouth opening to give the speech I readily *could* recite word for word now, but I held up my hand before she could even begin. Her mouth didn't close, but her features went slack in confusion.

"Mom," I said, "I have to talk to you. I'm not going to school today. I'm staying home, and so are you." She propped one slender boned hand upon her hip, raking the other through her tumbled red hair, two gestures combined that I knew very well. She was worried.

"What's going on Grace, are you sick?"

Oh, the replies I could have given. But this was going to be tricky. I had to tread lightly, otherwise I would be lying on an odd couch and listening to some dude with a monotone asking me questions to determine how high up my freak flag was flying. I closed the distance until I was close enough to grab the hand she'd propped on her hip. I took it in both of my own and looked into her weirdly wonderful violet eyes.

"You're going to think I'm crazy... but please, Mom, stay home, and listen to me. If not, bad things are gonna happen." *And they probably will anyway*, the voice in my head morbidly grumbled.

For a brief moment I wished that it were Amy standing in front of me instead of mom. Amy with her dirty blond hair, pin straight, and fashionably cut, that curled out at her jaw-line at the tips. She was the opposite of me in so many ways, but we had a bond that had stood strong since kindergarten. She always, and I mean always, dressed to kill. Not slutty, exactly, but provocative enough to make your green eyed monster pop up if she so much as sniffed in your boyfriend's direction. She was all curves and long French manicured nails. Her bright blue eyes lit a face that had never suffered the woes of hormonal breakouts. I envied her at times, and wanted to smack her at others, especially when she came out with something anal and self absorbed. But she was the most loyal person I knew. She'd never betrayed me in my secrets, and never blew me off when I felt particularly crappy. I loved her. But this wasn't something I could involve her in. Not something her fashion crammed brain could comprehend, or want to. I couldn't burden her. I kept pretty quiet, I didn't gossip much, and unlike her, I didn't feel the need to run the show. Looking at it from my current predicament, I realized I'd never come to her with any major issues. I'd never whined to her about any of my problems, it just wasn't my style. She also had this horribly practical side, and no belief in anything beyond what she could see. She would likely laugh and say that my problems were stress related, brought on from my horrible breakup with Adam. Confiding in her would only result in my resisting the urge to strangle her.

But my mom wouldn't laugh at me, and, though I felt that Amy was trustworthy, I would never run the risk of having her label me "psycho" and telling the whole school that I did mind-altering drugs. I hated to admit it, but Amy could be a total bitch if you somehow got under her golden tanned skin. There was my mother, standing before me with a look that told me I had her attention and support. That look told me she'd love me and do anything to help me, no matter how crazy I sounded. This was the same lady that had entered my room every night for four months when I was seven, shining a cheap dollar store flash light under my bed and into my closet to assure me the shadow monster wasn't there lurking – waiting to eat me up as soon as the lights went out. So I decided to break open the dam. I squeezed her hand and met her eyes, those weirdly beautiful violet eyes. "Please, just trust me, mom. I'm in trouble... and..."

"Oh *my* God," she lowered her head for a brief moment and then looked back up at me. And with the worry that wrinkled her forehead I saw something else in her expression, anger. "Is it

Adam? Has he hurt you? Grace, oh, *honey*, please tell me that he didn't? I mean... tell me if he did, because I'm going to kill him. Has he... Oh – oh God, are you pregnant Grace?"

I shook my head quickly, "No, nothing like that. Geez, *Mom*," and I realized I was squeezing her hands hard enough to hurt her because she flinched. I softened my grip, "Mom, it's nothing like that. I promise. Please, just trust me ok?" She lowered her head again but this time she didn't look back up. Instead she breathed deeply through her nose, and out of her mouth, shutting her eyes, her own mini meditation she used in times of intense stress.

"Okay," she said.

Normally she would have asked me a million questions. Normally she would have pinned me there on the spot and demanded an explanation. But something in my voice, something in my eyes, must have conveyed the importance of her open silence. But first, I needed to gather my wits.

"Mom, I need a hot bath. Just go downstairs and I'll be there in a few minutes. I'll hurry, okay?" She raised her head and I saw her uncertainty. But she nodded anyway, so I turned and left her standing there in my room and quickly walked into the adjoining bathroom.

The first thing I did was clear the clutter of shampoo bottles on the side of the tub. I had this horrible habit of leaving them scattered everywhere and rarely returned them to the shower hanger. I scanned the tub for anything that could be possibly menacing. I found a disposable razor sitting beside a bar of the peach scented soap I had sloppily left outside of the dish, and plunked it into the wastebasket beside of the toilet. I doubted anything bad would happen in my harmless bathroom, but still, this was a game, and he could always have an unexpected play up his sleeve. I ran the water hot, just how I like it. I didn't even wait for the tub to fill before I stripped off my pajamas and eased in. I sighed, feeling my muscles loosen considerably. Now, it was time to get my stuff straight.

I had decided to tell her everything (leaving out the parts of his cheek licking and my sick puppy reaction), and tried to imagine how it would sound if our roles were reversed. I knew how it would sound to me, to anyone, really. So how could I convince her? I also battled with the knowledge that telling her would not likely be helpful. What did I expect her to do with this burden on her shoulders? How would my telling her help anything in the long run? I tried telling myself that I wouldn't be telling her for selfish reasons – to have someone to share my fear and confusion with – but that was, sadly, a lie. I didn't want to be alone in this. But I also didn't want to drag the person I loved most in the world into my hellish battle. I was trying to get my thoughts in order and recall all of the events of the last couple of days when I felt it, a stinging sensation on my outer right ankle.

"Ouch, what the hell?" I said out loud between clinched teeth I felt it twice more, like little taps of fire in the same area. I pulled my right knee to my chest, tilting my head and trying to find a wound of some sort. The area was red, and in the center there were three tiny dots, almost in a perfect triangle. As I watched, three little dots of blood beaded on my skin. A wasp sting, maybe? I frowned, intending to hunt out my new enemy when I heard a noise.

I looked up, my heart constricting, and saw exactly what had made that noise. Kracious sat on the toilet at my feet, directly to the right. He tipped a boyish smile and gave me a look of lustful appreciation. He clapped his hands slowly like a music snob in the audience of a classical composition. I quickly pulled both knees to my chest in an attempt to hide my nakedness and shot him the dirtiest look I could muster. His lips were pressed together and he emitted a low snorting sound. He closed his eyes, trying to compose himself, and quickly opened them. "Hi, bay-beh," he said, letting his giggles escape, which were deceptively musical and pleasant to the ear.

"Get out!" I whispered savagely.

I didn't want to alert my mother. I wanted to fill her in, but I didn't want to give her the awful shock treatment by discovering a hot dude with black eyes watching her teenage daughter bathe. I also didn't want to risk her getting hurt. I knew he certainly wasn't above playing dirty, so I did some internal cursing and a whole lot of mental screaming. I gasped as the stinging sensation in my ankle became a persistent burn. I let my left hand slide down my injured leg to cradle the area. I could feel the swelling, and heat that was rapidly spreading to both my foot and lower calf. I gritted my teeth to keep from crying out.

Kracious titled his head back and inhaled, his lips parting, and then, slowly, he looked back down at me. His legs were crossed, and his foot bounced cheerily in the air. He crossed his arms and gave me what would have been with anyone else, a disarming grin.

"I do enjoy watching a lady bathe," he purred.

I looked down and saw it floating there, aha! All I had handy was a thoroughly soaked sponge, but I grabbed the dripping mass and threw it as hard as I could manage without giving him a peep show. But he was gone. *Poof.* Hot demonic sorcerer, vanished. Then I felt something pinch me and looked down at my feet with my legs still pressed to my chest. I began to scream, and would have fainted had my need for flight not been so strong. The thing had made its way onto my toes with its panicked little spidery legs. It had obviously been trying to avoid drowning and I realized then what had left such a horrible burning on my ankle.

It was an odd orange in color and tiny, not even the length of my pinky finger. My mother burst in just as I was scrambling out with my hands waving in the air, screaming at the height of my lungs capacity. I stood there naked, jumping in place, and shrieked as I pointed towards the tub, but my mother only looked blank and confused. When she finally followed the direction of my point, her look of disbelief was so profound it would have been comical under any other circumstances.

CHAPTER 6

Numb Revelations

We both shrieked as she swished the scorpion into a mason jar, then, tilting it against the metal of the tub, she allowed the water to pour back out, capturing the little horror inside. The ride to the hospital was brief and painful. The scorpion struggled to climb the sides of the jar unsuccessfully while it rode in a mason jar in a cup holder in between us in the console. Despair mingled with the pain as I lay my head against the head rest.

Just so happens, one of the ER nurses happened to be a huge scorpion buff. His expression was one of awe as he tapped the mason jar and spoke in that whispery tone that reminded me of a twelve year old comic book buff that's looking at a rare first edition Batman comic. The pain was extending to my pelvis, but what bothered me even worse was the fact that my leg was slowly going numb, as if falling asleep. The doctor, an Indian man with a last name I could only tell you starts with a *B* and would take an hour of practicing to pronounce correctly, listened to him intently. The doctor occasionally spoke to another middle aged woman in white scrubs. She nodded often, her brown hair expertly wound at her nape in a tight bun. She was perfectly composed and had a no-nonsense vibe, but I noticed her lips curled down in disgust as she watched the scorpion tink around the jar. It held up its small pinchers, tense with agitation, hungry to sting again. My mother was trying her best to keep from crying as she listened to the male nurse prattle on.

"It's a Death stalker scorpion. Normally you'll find them in Africa or the Middle East, but really, anyone can buy them and keep them. It's legal, but certainly not the smartest pet to keep. He's not cuddly." He tapped the jar for emphasis and the scorpion struck the glass, quick as lightning with his fat orange tail. He didn't flinch, but I did. "He's probably someone's pet, hard to find such a tiny little thing if they go missing." I knew my mother was wondering which of our neighbors would keep such a dangerous pet, but I knew who he belonged to. And he just so happened to wear lots of leather. The male nurse went on. "I know a guy that bought one on the Internet and had the bright drunken idea to balance one on his nose. Let's just say he hasn't been the same since…"

His voice dropped low and he gave the doctor a meaningful glance that I suppose was meant for him only. I caught on – and so did my mom – because she whimpered softly and pressed the back of one shaking hand to her lips. I sat on the exam table and tried to keep from squirming at the hot pain growing stronger with each minute. I reached over and squeezed her shoulder, wishing like hell that I could ease her fear, but I was too consumed by my own to be much of a comfort. I had begun to get chills and I tried unsuccessfully to keep my teeth from chattering. The nurse suddenly cradled the jar to his chest like a five year old taking his pet kitten for a stroll and motioned for the doctor to follow him from the room. I struggled to make out the doctors words through his thick, beautiful accent.

"We're going to make some calls. *John* – the nurse you just met – is a scorpion enthusiast as I'm sure you can tell. Based on what we know, we're going to search for an anti-venom. Don't fret, we'll find someone who supplies here in the US. Our only issue is time, because from what John tells me, we'll need to find one fast."

The lady in the white scrubs popped a thermometer into my mouth and it beeped softly after just a moment. "103.1," she said quickly, and the doctor nodded as he left the room. "I'll be back shortly, but please, tell the nurse if you experience any changes," he told my mother.

My mom hit the doc with at least twenty-one questions before they left, but I couldn't focus on his answers. After he left, I examined my ankle and bit my lip to keep from exclaiming at the swelling. My foot was the size of a Volkswagen. Taking my mother's advice, I lay down; but it did no good. I rolled and panted with the pain as it traveled the length of my body. The burning, – or what felt more like melting – had reached my chest and was radiating down one arm. My mother's tears flowed freely as she rubbed my back. I had turned so she couldn't see my face. I didn't want her to see the agony there.

"Cold," I told her, and like magic the nurse appeared with fever reducer, a warmed blanket, and a tiny paper cup filled with water. It was hard to swallow the bitter round pill, because my throat keep constricting with pain. I had an awful suspicion that the anti-venom – if found at all – would not appear on time. The nurse had also said that even a single string from that particular scorpion could be deadly if left untreated, and I'd been stung a whopping three times. I concluded that I would tell my mother as much as I could about what was happening. If I had to go into the dark, I didn't want to go with so much horrific knowledge. I needed her advice. She'd likely think me delusional, but it was worth a shot.

"Mom..." I rolled over and began, gasping through waves of white hot pain. "I need you to know what's happening, I'm not delusional, whatever my fever. This is all the truth. Just listen... no questions. We don't have much time. Ok?"

I was seriously proud of her, because she only insisted I rest once. After that, I had her total attention. It was a slow process because every ten minutes someone was coming inside and checking my pulse, or my temperature. The doctor also visited quite often, even though the ER had appeared quite busy earlier. His voice betrayed his cautiously blank expression, and I could hear the worry there. They hadn't been able to find a supplier yet, and they were moving me to a room in intensive care. As soon as he left to give the order I managed to finish my story, leaving out the more perverse details, like my strange attraction to Kracious. I heard the doctor speaking of "incubation" as I pretended not to overhear. This was going to be bad, really bad. Why couldn't someone just shoot me in the head again? I'd prefer that any day to the agony of my swollen body. My skin was beginning to bleed in some places where the swelling was more pronounced. It was actually cracking open; with the fluid that was trying to painfully find its way out.

I didn't meet her eyes throughout the story, and several times I had had to stop and cry out with misery. By the time they were moving me to intensive care the numbness was taking over. My entire body might as well have been covered in ice cubes. My teeth chattered as they hooked me up to several beeping monitors and injected fresh pain killers into the IV in my limp, numb arm. My mother came to my bedside and pressed her forehead against mine. Talking was too much effort, so I kept quiet. No need for her possibly last memory of her daughter alive to be of my slurred speech. "Oh honey... I don't know... I just don't know... but you have to fight this. I'm here baby, I'm here. No one's going to hurt you. They're going to get the anti-venom and we're going to go back home. No one's going to hurt you."

She didn't believe me, of course, she thought me crazy. But during the few short hours that followed with her rocking and weeping at my bedside ,she told me a story; her voice thick with hopeless pain.

"When you were little, you were playing in Gran's yard. You couldn't have been more than five years old, and you found this little toad." She paused, sniffling to no avail, her nose was clogged. But her voice was steady as she continued. "You brought it to her there on her porch, and said 'Look Granny, he doesn't have to bump the ground anymore when he hops, now he can fly.'" She went silent for a moment, but continued. I noticed – not for the first time – how her soft, charming country accent was more pronounced when she was sad. I wondered why she was telling me this. But my mother knew, she wasn't dumb, nor was she someone to delude herself with false hopes. She knew I was dying. And this was apparently important. "The little toad had wings, Grace. Real wings, but even though that's impossible, it wasn't even the strangest thing. His wings were pink, and gauzy. They sparkled like the fairy's wings in that movie you loved so much, *Peter Pan*." A sob broke through. "Your grandmother and I were amazed and even a little delighted by it, but we weren't after we asked you about it. You told us 'I wanted him to have them, and there they were.'"

"I never asked what your grandmother did with the toad, but she took it out back. It kept trying to hop away, and managed once, and it flew a little. And whenever it flew, bright glitter puffed out in every direction, like a special effect on some fantasy flick. Your grandma's hands were sparkling when she came back. She never told me... or you, for that matter, what she'd done with it." She met my eyes and I nodded with great effort. *Go on* I wanted to convey. *I need this.* She got the message, and did.

"After that more things happened, each just as strange as the toad. In the dead of winter you went out to that climbing rose vine on the side of the house, you always loved it." I knew which one she referred to. It was beautiful when it bloomed in the summer. "It was winter and it was just a scraggly looking old vine, not a hint of green. You were maybe seven then, and you asked me if I wanted to see the roses. I went outside with you, knowing full well that there weren't any in bloom, and I was right, there weren't. The vine was bare. But then you touched it and whispered something I couldn't make out-" She paused, catching her breath, and her chest heaved. I knew this was painful for her. But my head was reeling. *Go on!* I wanted to scream. Finally, a shred of hope!

She went on. "It bloomed beneath your hand. It became green and buds popped up and burst open and then the roses... the prettiest roses I've ever seen. And there are so many other little things, Grace. Little things I've never told you. Things I preached at you to forget; and I guess you did, because you've never mentioned them yourself. You had a gift, an amazing gift. And it scared me."

Time was running out, my breathing was getting a little labored, and I wanted to hear it all. I wanted to know everything. She didn't disappoint. "The Dotson's weren't always there... and years ago another family lived there – the Connar's – and they had a little boy about your age. You rode the school bus together, you sat together in class, I guess he was sort of like your fourth grade sweetheart."

I wanted to smile at his memory. I've been madly in love with Tommy Connar and had vowed passionately many times that I would marry him as a child. I never knew what had happened to him, it was like one day, he'd just vanished. I'd taken it pretty hard, pining for him like any maiden for her knight.

Mom kept going. "One day Tommy came over and announced that he and his family were leaving for Florida for an extended stay with his Grandparents for a couple of months. You asked to go with him, of course, and you took it pretty rough. Then you became angry, a natural reaction to sadness in a child Grace – remember that." At this point she was crying so hard that I struggled to comprehend her through the growing numbness and foggy clouds in my head.

"So you... you told Tommy. 'I hope a shark eats you.'" A groan escaped me. I didn't want to hear the rest. "A week later Tommy was swimming on a beach that rarely ever had reported shark sightings, it was considered to be one of the safest in that area. But there was one attack, and it happened to be on Tommy. He ended up losing his leg."

I let it sink in, along with guilt, old guilt and old memories that were suddenly surfacing.

"It was then that I drilled it into your head, I guess it was a sort of brainwashing, and I'm sorry baby. *I am sorry*, but I was afraid that eventually someone would realize what a gift you had, and take you away from me. I told you to forget. I told you never to make things happen again. I told you it was bad. And I worried. I worried that others would get hurt. But what happened to Tommy wasn't intentional, Grace. It wasn't, and you mustn't blame yourself for it. You were a child; a baby, really. Just think, how many times does the average human wish ill will on another on a daily basis? It's human. It's darkness, yes, but we all walk in it sometimes."

She put her hands into her hair and began to rock, her voice was thick, and I was able to turn my head enough just so I could look down at her. Tears dripped from the tip of her small nose and were quickly absorbed by her jeans. "But eventually you forgot, and it stopped, all of the... special things. It stopped, and after a while it was like you'd never been touched by whatever entity had saw fit to make you something more than everyone else."

I was reeling. In spite of the pain, the numbness, and confusion brought on by the poison pumping through my veins, I felt sick inside on a new level. Suddenly what she had told me had manifested into memories. I could feel a dam breaking, and old pain washed around me, chilling me to the bone.

My mom's voice sounded far away. "I still don't want to believe. But at the same time, it's my only hope. Grace, earlier, I heard his voice. I'd never left your room. For a minute I thought – I thought that maybe it was Adam. I was going to storm the door... but you screamed before I did. But then... there was no man... no Adam... no more voice. Grace, who was he?" I couldn't answer her. I couldn't give her anymore. I was fading. But I'd told her already. And then suddenly she was beside of me, laying her head gently across my chest, directly above my heart. My breathing had taken on a new sound – a deeper, slower sound – almost like a snore. I listened as if from far away, but I heard what she said as black crept around the corner of my vision.

"If what you say is true, you'll come back... you'll come back to me. Won't you? You'll come back. I need to believe it. It's all I have, or I won't make it through this night. And you have to fight him. You have to call on whatever it is you have inside, whatever drew him to you, and you have to beat him. I love you"

CHAPTER 7

Savior

I could feel a tear slide down my cheek and I could smell the faint lingering scent of dog shampoo. I wanted to hold her. I wanted to tell her I would return. But perhaps Kracious was bored with me. Maybe the game was growing cold. One of the machines began beeping and I was faintly aware of my mother being rushed from the room. And then it happened again. I became aware. I was numb, yes, but for a moment, I wasn't dying. My brain shook off the fog and my mind began racing. I waited to see the mysterious douche-bag's smiling face above me and wished I could still spit. But I couldn't sense his darkness. I couldn't feel the newly familiar dread that always reached me before I spotted him.

Instead, it was light; light, and warmth. Alarm raced through me. Maybe I wasn't going to meet Kracious-the-whatever-the-hell-he-was on whatever plane I saw him on last. Maybe I was passing into another life. Maybe God was pulling me into his arms. I suddenly felt comforted by the thought. In church my Gran used to sing of golden streets and a place where every tear would be wiped from her eyes. I would have peace. But a man's voice reached my ears, and although beautiful, I knew it wasn't the voice of the almighty.

"Ma'am, I need you to step out. I'm going to do everything I can."

Then suddenly the door was being slammed. I could hear knocking and shouts – more than my mother – a few people. What was happening? I could hear the word "security" amid the shouting, along with my mother screeching my name.

The man that suddenly leaned over me was the opposite of my new nemesis. Where Kracious was dark beauty; this man was golden perfection. His eyes were the color of those turquoise oceans you only see on postcards. His lashes were thick and

black, his brows, in a natural arch that made him look wise. His
nose, much like Kracious', was strong and roman-like, but the
resemblance stopped there. A full mouth was set in a frown that
took nothing away from his hotness. Yes, hotness being the key
word here. If Brad pit were to have an almost identical twin in
"*Troy,*" he would be it. A jagged scar ran, white and thick from
the outer corner of his eye to mid cheek. But the scar didn't
diminish his beauty; it only served to give him an edge. His
golden hair brushed his shoulders and as he leaned over, some of
it fell into his eyes. He pushed it back and met my gaze, and if I
would have had the ability, I would have gasped in wonder.

I would have also jumped and hung to the ceiling with my
claws like a cartoon cat with his sudden outburst.

"You reek of him!" he almost spat the words, his frown
settling even firmer.

I waited, wondering if he were going to power bomb me and
send me flying into the wall. No way I could protest, let alone
put up a fight. He just sounded *so* pissed. His voice was deep,
gravelly, and very cowboy. His accent was one I couldn't place.
He bowed his head for a moment, and when he lifted his head
his voice was more controlled. I watched him make a visible
effort to relax his features.

"I smelled it from the street, his magic; like a corpse too long
in the sun."

And then another emotion played across his expressive face;
sympathy. Sympathy and something else I couldn't put my
finger on. I wanted to hold him. A face like his should never have
anything other than a smile. He reached out a huge hand and
placed it on my forehead. He stood to his full height then –
which was massively tall. He reminded me of a mountain; a
super hot mountain that everyone no doubt wanted to climb. I
chastised myself. Here I was, dying *again,* and all I could do was
picture him in a loin cloth. But it wasn't just attraction. I wanted
to comfort him. I wanted to wipe the worry from the face of this
beautiful, freaky stranger. Something radiated from him, and
the only word I had to describe it was *goodness.*

He spoke again. "You smell of something else too, your own
magic. But it's weak. And I don't think it will help you now." He
bent down once again and met my eyes, brushing hair from my
brow which I could only imagine looked like a Don King wig. He
continued, "I will try to help you. He cannot be allowed to

continue such things. You're but a child." His voice softened further on the last word. I wanted to disagree, but to him, that had to be what I was; a child. How old was he? Once again, I was staring up at a man that seemed ageless. But I was guessing he was perhaps 19 or 20. I breathed in, numb, but alert. His skin was of course, perfect. It was smooth and poreless, but unlike Kracious', it didn't seem wrong. He wanted to save me! I wanted to smile at him – to show my gratitude – but he obviously had some invisible remote, or whatever magical folks like Kracious used, and had placed me on pause. But then another thought occurred to me. What if he wasn't real? What if the scorpion's sting had induced a clever hallucination in my delirium? Or even worse, what if this was Kracious' sick idea of a joke? I began to mentally whimper. I wanted to shut my eyes but they were glued open, staring at the hottest being on the planet that could very well be the most evil in disguise. Not that Kracious wasn't gorgeous, but, come on, he'd forced me to wake up in a repetitive hell everyday and killed me freakishly sometime during each. But then the blond man spoke.

"I have read you. I have seen your deaths. Such pain..." His hand pressed down more firmly on my forehead and he shut his eyes, his lips twitching at the corner in what appeared to be disgust. "I can break the spell, but it would not do to have everyone here see you cured this day. Something so miraculous would gain much attention. Not to mention, I will be under suspicion, and the authorities were never favorites of mine."

So what are you going to do? I wanted to question, and his head shot up. He met my eyes.

"We are going to take you back to a time before; before the sting. Your mother has knowledge of what you were once capable of, but she knows nothing more. She doesn't know how to help you. Do not talk to her. She won't remember any of what had transpired this day. Rise and go to the place where you learn."

I thought about this and decided that he could only be talking about school.

He went on, "On your bed you will find an amulet. Wear it. It will link us. I will know when you are in danger. "He bent down close to my ear and I could feel his warm breath tickling the nape of my neck as he spoke, "After your studies, do not go with the others on the... bus." The word "bus" sounded like a word he wasn't used to using. I could also detect a hint of distaste as he spoke it. "You are to meet me in the center of town, at the novelty shop. You should know where that is, it is the only one of its kind in this area."

I did. Although I'd only been in there once with Adam who had a thing for *"The Punisher"* comics. The place had everything from comics to magic kits. It was also rumored that the so-called Wiccan chicks of our school were fond of shopping there, due to the secret "room" that supposedly housed supplies needed for advanced witchcraft in the back. I tried to nod, but to no avail. His weird telepathy must have picked it up. I was suddenly horrified as I remembered picturing him in a loin cloth.

He suddenly threw back his head and laughed. "That is not how it works, little one. I have to touch you, first. And not just anywhere," He gave a little smile." I must have contact with your third eye." I was assuming that was somewhere on my head. He withdrew his hand and I wished I could move so I could crawl under the hospital bed and die. But my embarrassment was short lived and replaced by warmth as he gently took my shoulders. It was then that I became aware of something crashing at the door and a woman's voice – who sounded suspiciously like my mother – screeching in rage and fear.

He soothed, "They cannot enter, but your mother is in much distress. It's time to go, little one. You're very close now, and if you're lost now, I cannot bring you back."

I remembered how Kracious had sealed my fate with a kiss, and feverishly wished that this man would do the same. I wanted to ask for his name. I wanted to see how it felt rolling off of my tongue. But my tongue wouldn't work, and my mom was gonna have a heart attack if we didn't do something fast.

"Remember the amulet," was all he said before I was racing; racing backwards and watching the events of the day race by at a sickening speed. I relived the slow paralysis, the pain, the sting, and my heartbreak as I watched my mother cry. I relived the horror of seeing the scorpion for the first time. I watched Kracious smiling at me from the porcelain throne, all of it. But it raced by much too quickly to be *too* torturous.

And suddenly, I was waking again. But this time I practically bolted up like there was a spring attached to my back. I frantically searched the bed for the amulet and almost screamed with relief when my hands touched something cool and smooth. I picked it up and greedily took in its beauty. It was made of what appeared to be silver, around the size of a silver dollar. It felt surprisingly heavy as I held it in my palm. I gasped at the intricate design. It was in the shape of a cross – but the texture and effect was that of a tree – a twisting tree with branches entwined with one another. It was silver, and at the end of each branch – on the points of the tiny limbs – were twinkling diamonds. In the center was an oval shaped stone, black as night, but when I ran my thumb across it, it began to glow with a soft, white light that warmed my hand as I cautiously closed my hand over it. I could almost feel him, whoever he was, and I wanted to cry with gratitude. A hope was building inside of me, but I didn't want it to bloom out of control only to wither and be ripped apart. I let it take root, nonetheless. I quickly draped it over my neck and instantly felt it grow even warmer, feeling delicious and strengthening against my chest.

CHAPTER 8

Forget the Bus

I glanced at the clock and saw that it was once again 7:30. I was in the same pajamas which by normal standards should be totally rank by now – but this type of morning didn't exactly call for detergent and worry over the state of my clothing. In reality... or... err... whatever, this was the first night I had worn this particular sleepwear. I heard my mother's feet quickly padding up the stairs and was out of bed before she could burst through the door.

"Yes mom, I know, yes, I have a test, yes, I'm going to be late. I'll shower quickly and yes, you need to put on some pants. The grocer doesn't need to see your Betty Boop roos, he may enjoy that a little too much."

She gaped at me as I walked into the bathroom with a grin. But as soon as I shut the door I peered around anxiously. No way was I taking a bath today. I wasn't going anywhere near that tub. I knew that Kracious would appear on the throne in about five minutes, so I ran a brush through my hopeless waves and bolted out as quickly as I could. I didn't even look at my clothing as I jerked it out of the closet and put it on. It wasn't until my mother and I were driving that I looked down to confirm I wasn't wearing that god-awful *Spice Girls* tee shirt that I had worn to paint my room in and sighed with relief. Instead it was a plain black tee which went fine with my faded jeans and pink sneakers. Funny, that I should be worrying about my outfit when an evil sorcerer was plotting my death. I got a couple of odd looks from my mother when I cautioned her twice to drive carefully – I didn't want to take any chances. When we passed old man Gerry's farm I tensely yelled, "Watch out for cows!" which earned me one of her best ever "WTF" looks. Who knew what could happen?

I found it easier to concentrate on my test, although the day was predictable as usual. I tried not to be totally freaked out by it, but that was sort of impossible. I did have the decency to tell Tabitha Hanley to turn off her cell phone at the beginning of Mrs. Stacy's biology class, earning me a weird, cautious look as she reached into her bag to grab it and turn it off. I finished my test early, confident on my *A*, and was the first to Mrs. Stacy's desk. I sat down and took advantage of remaining twenty minutes of class. Now was the time to think.

Okay, so I had one super hot evil sorcerer that wanted to kill me over and over and possibly eat my soul. The other, whom I was guessing was the equally hot *good* sorcerer, or wizard, or *whatever*, somehow knew of Kracious' weird fascination with me and wanted to help me put a stop to his reign of terror. Sexy Merlin (without the long white beard and frail frame, which is what I had named him in my head since he'd failed to tell me his name), had somehow gotten his hand on the wheel of time and spun me back to my morning bed. I was currently wearing a beautiful amulet which he claimed would somehow allow him to know when I needed him, sort of like the Batman signal, I guessed. That sort of distracted me and I began to think of him clad in leather and jumping from buildings and I mentally spanked myself for getting horribly off track with my recap.

He was going to try to stop the curse with some magic of his own. This, I assumed, would royally piss Kracious off. He stuck me as the type that didn't like his work tampered with. He had claimed me, and Sexy Merlin was stepping into his territory. I didn't think this would end in hugs and apologies on his part. I wasn't expecting to get roses when I got home with a note that said, "Sorry for killing you twice, good thing you didn't die the third time. Let's have lunch sometime." No, I saw a hard road ahead and I would have to be on my toes the entire time. Death could come from any direction. I stiffened. How could I function this way? I've watched the show (much to my mother's disappointment) *"1,000 ways to die,"* and I'm pretty sure there are a lot more than that. How would I even be able to sleep at night? What if he was waiting outside of the door right now?

I then went over what my mother had told me and opened myself to the memories that I had buried so long ago. I remembered the frog with wings. I had been thinking about the fairy tale with the frog prince. Somehow I had also confused that with Tinker bell, or something similar. I don't remember doing anything in particular. I couldn't, I was far too young and my memory isn't that super. But I remembered the horror on mom's face, and my Grandma's firm jaw as she carried the tiny feathered thing back behind the house. No doubt to destroy it.

Then I thought about the shark and Tommy – Tommy, who had moved away to Florida permanently after that. Had I really caused the shark attack? Was I the cause of his permanent disability? I remember him coming in whenever I was twelve. They'd been in town to visit some family. I'd noticed him walking fine and wrapped my arms around him as he'd come through the door, noticing with delight that he'd turned into a super cute pre-teen. He was walking but my heart sank when he lifted his pant leg to reveal the metal artificial limb beneath with the curved piece of metal that served as his foot. Then, I'd had a flicker of memory – of guilt – but I couldn't remember cursing him. Now I did, and that wound had been reopened. I remembered trying to hard to forget, to forget that I was special. I remembered my mother hammering into my head that I could never do anything of the sort ever again. Not with frogs, fish, or people. Not with anything. She preached this in a frenzied manner that was almost creepy in its intensity. It bordered on cruelty, without her ever lifting a hand. It had eventually sunk in. I associated whatever it was that I could do with "bad." She told me to forget, and forget I did.

Where had it come from? My father? Surely not. If he were that unique he wouldn't have been in a lame Elvis cover band. I didn't want to think about it anymore. I didn't want to accept that I was indeed a freak. But I would have to save my current self disgust for a time (if it ever came) when my life wasn't hanging in the balance. I would try to remember it all later. If later ever came.

I glanced toward the door but tried to relax, telling myself that I would sense Kracious if he were this close. I had to talk to someone. And by someone I mean someone that isn't all magical and cryptic. But who would ever believe me? Not Amy, but God, how I missed her. How I wished she could understand. I simply had to talk to her, to enjoy a few moments of brainless chatter, but not about this. Adam? No. Adam might have been an extremely good kisser and he had the cutest butt in all of Birchhound, but beyond closing the fridge door over and over,

trying to figure out the exact moment when the mysterious
fridge light came on, he wasn't into the mysterious.

And then it hit me. He was the school outcast, for sure. The
undisputed, official, Birchhound nerd leader. He was what
everyone liked to call "The school loser," but I'd always been nice
to him. I'd always kinda wanted to invite him to eat lunch with
Amy and my equally sort-of-stuck-up group of friends but knew
that they would only verbally eat him alive. He was constantly
shuffling a set of *Dungeons and Dragons* cards nearly every time
I'd ever seen him, even while walking. The only time I'd seen
him smile was on Halloween, when he'd come to school dressed
as a Hobbit, which – Oh God – was a disaster. He was heedless
to the snickers and evil jabs from our jocks, looking confident
and happy with his hairy fake feet and black curly wig. He'd also
sported a huge faux golden ring that actually glowed if he
pushed a tiny button on the side.

He and his fellow nerds were quite a sight, the tallest of the
three being Shane Tiller, whom had dressed up as the wizard. I
remembered passing them in the hall and hearing them
replicating the weird LOTR accents perfectly and rolling my
eyes. They were just so into it. And I was confident they would
all die virgins. The three of them were like peas in a pod, and
just about as appealing with their social skills. Come to think of
it, I'd never seen them actually speak to another soul outside of
their group unless forced to do so. They were just, well, *weird*.
Most kids suspected them to be gay, but my instincts suggested
otherwise. The gay kids at my school we're usually comfortably
open about their sexuality. Time's had changed, and even in
backwoods Birchhound, people weren't ignorantly homophobic
like they used to be.

On Halloween we were allowed to wear our costumes to
school, providing they weren't too over the top. Last year I had
dressed as a 40's chick in a sequined dress and a short blonde
wig. I'd thought it was cute and tasteful. Stank-ho Ericka had
had the nerve to dress up as a showgirl, her butt cheeks hanging
out with feathers seeming to sprout from the small of her back.
Her boobs were barely contained in the silver strapless one piece
that might as well have been a nightie. Every time some
hormonal guy would cat-call at her costume she would strike a
pose and kick out one tan leg, displaying her four inch heels. I

had wanted to rip off her feathered headdress and beat her with it.

I had a new partner in crime in mind, someone that might believe me. He just didn't know it yet.

Chad Felix.

CHAPTER 9

Breaking the Rules

It seemed like only a minute had passed when the bell rang. I made my way out into the hall and was greeted by Amy for the first time that day. Our first three classes had us pretty much on separate ends of the building, and we usually only sought each other out in between those classes if it were an emergency. An emergency as in *Oh my God did you hear that Sarah Gentry beat the hell out of Gretchen over that boy with the skull tattoo on his neck?"* Not, *"Holy shiznit an evil sorcerer saw me naked and put a scorpion in the tub this morning."*

She stood there; long and leggy in a faded blue jean mini with little blue gems around the hem. She was wearing her favorite pink gap top with the built in bra that made her generous cleavage (which she flaunted and fluffed every morning in the school bathroom mirror) seem super model perfect. She wore a tiny pink headband in her dirty blonde hair and although the front was slick with gel, the back was curled to perfection. Her shoes, of course, were to die for, cute little ballerina flats that matched perfectly with the pink shirt and headband. She arched one perfectly plucked brow at me and nearly fell over when I suddenly hug-attacked her, nearly squeezing the life out of her.

"Ouch, uh, wow Grace, nice to see you too. Ouch! Babe, you're gonna have to let go before you break one of the nails I just got done yesterday. I love you but you're so not going to ruin such hand perfection."

I released her reluctantly, choking up a little and wiped at my eyes, "I'm sorry, it's just

"Adam, what a prick," she finished for me. We had known each other for so long that she could finish my sentences for me.

"Yeah," I lied. She patted my back carefully and then examined her nails with a quick fluid motion afterwards.

"Come," she said in a comic butler imitation. "We shall comfort you with crappy cafeteria brownies and you can help me figure out whatever the hell is going on with my iPhone."

I inwardly groaned and nodded. After tossing our books unceremoniously into our lockers, we made our way to the cafeteria. I picked at my food and listened to Amy's now familiar iPhone rant. I examined the three other girls that sat around us in our little circle. Sheila Back, a near clone of Amy but without the warm streak. Chelle Swanson, the exotic looking brunette with just enough Cherokee to make her the most appealing squaw at Birchwood, and Maggie White; the red headed fire cracker that never ran out of anything to talk about, or *anyone*, for that matter.

They vaguely nodded as if totally into listening to Amy bitch loudly about the evil crap band wallpaper on her phone but I could tell they were only being polite. I watched as Maggie looked up at me and I averted my eyes for a moment, pretending to zone out. I looked back up as she was nudging Chelle and whispering in her ear. I saw Chelle's dark brown eyes lock on me and her face remained neutral.

"We're not talking about you, Grace, we're talking about, uh, um, Erika. What a slut, geez, look at her." Maggie said, unable to hide the guilt in her voice.

Wow, lame save, Maggie, I thought. There might as well have been a cartoon thought bubble above their heads with me in the center. I highly doubted they were speaking of Erika although as if on cue she materialized in that moment. I watched Adam's eyes lock on mine and I turned my head away. I did not want to think of how he had looked at me with the gun in his hand yesterday, or today, or whenever it was. Did he really hate me? Or was it just Kracious' influence that had made him want to kill me?

I remembered the warm kisses we had shared mere weeks ago on my doorstep and decided that, no; Adam wasn't capable of such a thing. Sure, he was a cheating prick, but he wasn't a killer. The same guy that sang loudly to Toby Keith in his truck and made me want to tear my ears off with the annoyance of it would never hurt me in that way.

I was seventeen and told myself that if I made it another two weeks, I would finally try for my license. I had my learners permit and I must say that I was doing pretty darn well for a novice driver, even if my mother had left fingernail imprints in the dash in front of the passenger seat. Perhaps she could finally be convinced that I was a safe enough driver to try for my license. But just now I didn't even want to practice. I did NOT want to be behind the wheel of a moving vehicle. That just had "Ready for a helluva ride? Jump inside," all over it while Kracious still lurked about. Come to think of it, I didn't want to be in a car, period. I decided to walk the short mile to school for the remainder of his game.

I turned my head quickly and grabbed Amy's wrist which was flailing with rage – the iPhone squeezed in her hand hard enough to break it. It must have been pretty darn durable. "Amy, I need to go talk to Chad. I think he can help me figure out if an old comic of my mothers is... um... worth money."

"Do what?" she asked loudly and dramatically. She looked back at Sheila, Chelle, and Maggie for confirmation that she wasn't overreacting and seemed pleased when she saw their sneers of approval.

"You cannot converse with the geek squad. It is strictly forbidden with those of us who happen to value our coolness." She huffed and tossed the iPhone down on the table a little too roughly, causing the bubble gum pink cover to pop off and skitter across the table.

"Aww, shit," she said and picked it up. I patted her back and leaned in close so the other girls couldn't hear.

"I won't be riding the bus. I'm going to be walking home. I'm going to go talk to Chad now and – Amy – don't even think about gossiping about me to our fellow snot squad." I loved her dearly but had just about enough of her shallowness. Once upon a time, I had overlooked it, and was even amused by it. But my patience was running thin and it was occurring to me just how narrow minded my little group was. The girl I had known since kindergarten was about as deep as a desert puddle. I got up and heard an outraged Maggie whisper a disgusted *what-ever* and turned my back on them.

"She's being *so* weird!" I heard Chelle whisper a little too loudly. But I wasn't stupid.

It wasn't supposed to be a secretive whisper. This was how the girls worked. They occasionally ate their own if someone dared to go against the grain a little. And I wasn't exactly the most loved in the group. Sure, Amy adored me. Yes, the others liked me, But I knew they viewed me as the eccentric one; the one that's always on the brink of ejection from the herd. On another day I would have nervously bitten my nails at the thought of their rejection, but today I really couldn't give a crickets britches what they thought. Amy was loyal, yes, but if she caught scent of my turmoil, I wouldn't put it past her to convince everyone that I was taking acid if others started noticing my weirdness. She would save her reputation, no matter the cost, when it came right down to it.

I approached the boys' table cautiously as Chad looked up from his deck of weird cards which I assumed was *Dungeons and Dragons* or something equally dorky. His eyes registered me and a look of cautious astonishment crossed his face. I looked at the others. Shane Tiller, and Brock Keller and took them in. Shane looked at me through his shaggy red bangs. The rest of his hair hung limply to the middle of his back. His face was thin and drawn and covered with a multitude of freckles. His lips were thin, his eyes, massive and an unnerving blue. He wore a white tee with some type of weird band logo screaming a loud read across his chest. He was tall, a whopping 6'4" – and painfully thin – the boy had never had a chance.

Brock was the most colorful of the three. He wore a lime green long sleeved shirt that zipped all the way up to his jaw-line. His giant Mohawk was dyed black, with purple on the tips. His eyes were his best feature, a chocolate brown with dark lashes and thick brows. He had a piercing in his nose which looked like that you would see on some Spanish bull. His lips were full and pouty, his nose, small and perfect, almost like that of a girls. On each finger he wore a ring, most of them something like skulls or weirdly shaped mood rings. The most impressive was the huge silver wolf head ring on his right index finger. I guessed that it could bruise a jaw quite easily. He was the most handsome of the three, and could seriously rack in the ladies if he ditched the hawk and made new friends, but the air about him seemed to vibrate with negative energy.

Most were afraid of him, and I think the only thing that kept them from being beat up on a daily basis was the aura of danger that Brock emitted. I looked back to Chad. Short and boyishly built, his brown hair was cut neatly just above the shoulder. His eyes, brown as well, didn't have the smoldering quality of Brock's, but were gentle and seemed wise beyond his years if you looked into them for more than a second. His lips were neither full nor thin. His nose was small and his skin, a creamy white that most girls would kill for. He was in a plain white tee and jeans and could easily pass for the nice smart boy next door that always made the honor role. They were all seniors like me, but Chad didn't look a day over fifteen.

"Hi guys," I put on my most friendly smile, "Can I sit with you for a few minutes?" I saw each of them wrinkle their brows in confusion and look at one another with amused faces. Brock looked at me, sneered, and then used his foot to forcefully scoot back a chair, causing it to screech.

"And to what do we owe this honor, Princess?" he mocked.

"Dude shut up and eat already," Shane said in a low monotone.

Brock grinned as I shot him a look dirty enough to pollute the town's water supply for months. Chad cleared his throat after glaring at Brock and spoke up. "Sit down if you want. It's just, if you're here on some stupid dare from the super-bitch pack over there, you might as well forget it. Being stood up isn't funny, and no, I will not do your homework for you."

I opened my mouth to protest but closed it and thought better of it. Taking the bait that was so enticingly offered would not be a great way to seek Chad's advice. I rounded the table and sat down beside of Brock, holding my chin high and ignoring the horrified looks from my girlfriends across the room.

"They don't look very pleased with you," Chad said, his voice musical and soothing.

"No, I suppose they're not, but I don't care. Yes, I need your help, but no, it's not with homework," I said softly. I waited for him to shut me down but he merely turned his head and stared into my eyes for a moment before looking away.

"Just what do you want to know?" He asked, his voice almost testing in its tone.

"I think she came here on a quest for your root, man," Brock said cheerfully.

Shane popped a potato chip into his mouth, never looking up, and said, "She'll never find it, it's much too small."

I ignored the stupid penis jokes and the rude insinuations and nervously fidgeted with my hands. Without thought reached for the chain around my neck and pulled out the beautiful silver tree branch cross. I rubbed the black stone gently in my fingers, feeling it grow warm as I closed my hand over it. Chad suddenly tensed. I looked to my left and noticed that Brock was staring at me with an intensity that made my hair stand on end. Shane was biting his lower lip, looking between the two.

"Nice necklace..." Chad said slowly. "Can you move your hand so I can get a better look at it?"

I did as he asked, wondering why he took an interest. Had it been glowing? I hoped it hadn't. I heard Brock hiss through his teeth and suddenly Chad was picking the amulet gently from my hands and examining it. I noticed that a bead of sweat had formed on his forehead.

"Where did you get this? I mean... buy it?" I heard a soft sound and looked down as his deck of cards tumbled from his other hand into the floor, but he didn't seem to notice.

I spoke carefully, emphasizing each word "I didn't. It was a gift, from a friend... a very special friend. It's sort of like... my good luck charm."

He looked up at me and let his expression fall carefully blank. I glanced over and saw that Brock's hands were fisted on the table – Shane had put his hands on each side of his head, a look of dread playing across his unfortunate features.

"I see," Chad said.

"Which is sort of why I'm here," I went on, heedless to how weird I was coming off. "I need someone to talk to about my friend, and I thought maybe... maybe you and I could hang out a bit later, you know, discuss it further. I think, if anyone could understand, it would be you."

I didn't know where this was going, but judging by their strange reaction they knew something. I'd said hello to each of them maybe twice in my time here at Birchhound, I didn't know them from Adam, yet I was ready to trust them with a secret so outlandish it was certain to make me seem like a raving lunatic.

I watched as Chad glanced about the table and saw each of them nod tersely in agreement. "Meet us at the park tonight, around seven if you can. All three of us will be there. We'll hang out."

"Okay," I whispered. "I will. Thanks Chad."

I got up and walked back to my table, ignoring the questions coming from all three girls that seemed to run into one loud drone. Whenever the word *"Losers"* was spoken at least eighteen times, the bell finally rang; signaling the end lunch. The rest of the school day went by at a snails pace and in drama I felt like crying when we were told we would be doing a copycat of *High school musical*. We would be working on for the rest of the year. This made me want to throw a pencil at Mr. Salyer's head. I really hated that musical.

CHAPTER 10

You've Got to be Kidding Me

At the end of the day I ditched the bus and began my half mile journey to the center of town. The walk was pleasant enough and the air was just crisp enough to cool the fine sheen of sweat from carrying my book bag, but not cold enough to conjure a river of snot rolling from my nose. Huffing and puffing, I reminded myself I needed to work out more, but hey, my bag was almost as heavy as I was. It seemed almost every teacher had saw fit to ruin my day further by providing loads of homework. But I took comfort in its weight. It was something I was used to, something normal, and routine.

At last I'd reached it and I didn't give myself time to consider what might be lurking inside. However, I did take the time to smooth down my hair and reapply lip gloss. *Amy would have approved*, I thought, a little disgusted with myself. I was hoping that the scariest thing in there was *X-men figurines*. A tiny bell jingled as I pushed open the glass door to "Elonzo's collectibles and novelties." The name made me think of a Mexican restaurant. As soon as I walked in I noticed the huge divider that ran from floor to ceiling, about seven feet in length. Various advertisements for comics and card games – as well as retro horror movie posters – covered it. It completely blocked the view of the clerk's desk. I had thought it inconvenient when I'd came in with Adam once before, and thought of it as such again. It was certainly an odd place for such a thing. It completely blocked the sunlight from entering the shop. I walked around it and almost knocked over a spinning shelf that had various, colorful comics on it. I steadied it and walked directly to the glass encased counter which was shaped like an unused staple. Various geeky treasures were in neat rows behind the glass, a few of the figurines in poses of combat with one another. The man behind the counter looked amused and with a flourish gestured to the shop, "Welcome to Elonzo's, my lady, how may I assist you this fine evening?"

I took in his appearance. His hair was a close cropped buzz cut, and the little hair that remained, jet black. He had the palest skin I'd ever seen. His eyes were a strange hue of green and his features were the type that seemed they could never crunch up in annoyance or anger. I glanced at his hands which he'd folded neatly on the counter. His hands were pale and his skin; almost transparent. I expected to see veins, but I couldn't see any. The nails – perfectly manicured and girlishly long – managed to gleam in the shop's weak lighting. He wore a simple black tee and black jeans as well. I could see the top of his black combat boots peeking at me through the glass. His smile – although pleasant – left me unsettled.

"Um," I balked. "I'm here to see a man... he told me to meet him here. I don't know his name... but... he's blond, and, he has a scar, right here," I gestured to my face and traced an imaginary scar for emphasis from the corner of my eye to my jaw line.

The man's expression changed dramatically to one that didn't seem to fit. Suspicion and what I swore had to be menace suddenly made him frightening to behold. "And why – my dear – did he ask you to meet him here?" His hands tensed as he moved them palm down on the glass. I felt a tiny rush of fear and took a step back. It was then, oddly, that I noticed there were no windows in the shop.

"Because, I need his help," I said lamely. I knew he'd noted the way my voice shook as he leaned forward and inhaled deeply as if I were a strange flower. He was trying to scare me. Why? He smiled again but this time I noticed that his eyeteeth were suddenly pointed and elongated. I gasped and turned, intending to run like hell when I heard *his* voice.

"Zimon, stop your interrogation! Don't you see she's just a human child?"

I expected the man to look sheepish, but he only smiled at the golden tall man beside of him. I noticed the fangs were gone. His teeth once again appeared normal, "I was merely welcoming her, Jeremiah. Maybe you should have given her a name before you sent her wandering in here to pry."

Jeremiah rubbed his brow and gave Zimon an annoyed look. "Imbecile," he muttered, "I don't know how many centuries more I can know you before I stake you."

The creepy fanged man, who was now merely just a creepy man, chuckled softly. He stretched out his hand to me and, as I met his eyes, I felt my feet taking me forward. My eyes were locked with his, and no matter how much common sense screamed at me that I was insane, I gave him my hand. He bent down and pressed his ice cold lips to the back of my hand, rubbing my knuckles, all the while keeping his eyes locked with mine.

"My apologies, love. I am Zimon. And since this buffoon to my left has failed to give you a name by which to call him, I shall do him the honors. That is Jeremiah. I am pleased to meet your acquaintance. By the way... you smell simply divine." He laughed again as Jeremiah grabbed his collar and jerked him easily away, leaving me shaking my head to clear the fog the man's gaze had created.

"Fiend!" he shouted as – still laughing – Zimon gracefully walked away, disappearing behind a heavily beaded curtain behind the counter. I was finally able to drag my eyes from Zimon and resume my train of thought. I'd had far too many encounters with weird beings for the past few days, err, day and my head was reeling. Would there actually be a real tomorrow?

"What is Zimon?" My brain formed the word but I didn't dare let it sink in.

"Damn vampires, extremely obnoxious. A word of advice, don't look them in the eyes. That's how they lure in their prey." He advised with a shake of his head.

I gasped and instinctively pressed my hand to the side of my throat. He saw this and quickly assured me.

"Don't fear him. He'd not dare harm you in my presence; or outside of it. I've saved his hide more than once, even though I sometimes doubt the wisdom of my doing so." With this he grumbled, and I had a moment to take in his golden beauty. I noticed for the first time how tall her was. He was 6'3 if anything, with a body that couldn't have an inch of fat. He wore a tight black turtleneck made out of some type of velvety material. His pants were black leather, lacking in frill and fitting snugly. He looked up and met my eyes and I instantly looked away. I didn't dare stare into them for any longer than necessary, lest I fall into them. I trembled where I stood, still holding my neck and feeling like I'd walked into another universe – a universe where I was the alien one.

"Come around the counter. We have much to discuss. I promise I won't bite. And I refuse to let Zimon bite you, either... much." I backed up a step and he smiled fully, laughing softly. "I'm sorry. It was meant to be humorous but I forget you have just stepped under the veil. This is all very new to you."

I closed my hand around the amulet and followed him behind the counter and through the black beaded curtain. I expected the back to be a clutter of boxes and supplies, but instead it looked like a very comfortable living room. A tiny room veered off to the left that housed a glass counter that went completely around the room – only allowing a gap for you to walk through. A red colored light dangled from the ceiling making everything inside appear ominous. I couldn't see the contents of the cases. I followed Jeremiah into the living space and sat on a large plush black velvety couch directly across from Zimon, who was sprawled out boyishly in a recliner across from me. He was seemingly very interested in a game show on the huge flat-screen that seemed to dominate the back of the room. I glanced around and thought how ordinary everything looked. It could be any man's bachelor pad, aside from huge mental storage cabinet that looked like safety deposit boxes that covered the wall behind Zimon. I expected Jeremiah to stand and talk, he seemed far too formal and serious to plop down beside of me, but that's just what he did. He made himself comfortable and crossed his leg, his ankle resting on his knee. He pushed his hair back in a slow, relaxed gesture.

"Zimon runs the shop. I'm on a temporary stay. I don't live here... and neither does he. So if anyone ever tries to pry information from you, it won't do them any good to know about the shop. They already do." I just stared at him, and to keep my hands from trembling, I balled them up and squeezed them between my knees. He looked me in the eye. "Kracious is a very old, very clever warlock. And by clever, I mean he's very good with his craft. His insanity has killed any common sense he may possess. He's not used to suffering consequences for his actions."

"Wait, Warlock? He calls himself a sorcerer," I said, wanting a *real* title for the evil man I was up against.

"Warlock... Sorcerer... Shaman... all the same. It's all very misunderstood." Jeremiah said. I listened as he continued, trying not to stare at his full lips and think of anything other than the problem at hand. He went on, easing back as he talked. "He's been alone for years-decades-centuries, and has had much time on his hands. Occasionally he will find someone that amuses him, and toy with them, not unlike a cat swatting at a mouse with a broken spine."

I found myself not liking that analogy.

He went on, "For some reason he's decided he wants to toy with you, child, and perhaps that is in part because he senses what's inside of you, though it's dormant for the time being. Perhaps he's trying to lure it out. It's not often a natural witch is born. Of course, you have no mentor, and cannot possibly know how to conjure or control the power inside." He softly patted his chest for emphasis. "But I am just as old as he is, and almost as clever, I'd like to think. At least I've avoided completely being consumed by the dark, like Kracious."

I found my voice, although shaky. "So... you were just, born, this way? And how old are you, because, dude, you don't look much older than me, and neither does Kracious."

His face was unreadable. "Yes, in a way. I was born with the magic, much like yourself. But it becomes useless if not tended properly. The magic is like a flower, without the proper nourishment, it withers and fades. There are different types of warlocks – and witches. I'm not speaking of those which suddenly decide to open a spell book and call themselves "Wiccans." They are ineffective. They speak of the elements but have no control over them. They practice spells without the light to ignite them. They are not real. A real witch is born as such. We do not need to speak words to conjure fire or any other type of element. Spells are used, but not for manifesting. We do not serve a Goddess, we serve light and nature. We try to serve love and light with our spells – whenever we do use them – and in return love and light sustains us, not hate and terror. Curses... binding spells... most of it is connected with darkness, although some can be used to heal. A real witch can live a very long time. The magic feeds something within that keeps us young. It has been told that some have even lived a thousand years. But I won't reveal my true age... I still feel young, that's all that counts. Right, Zimon?"

He paused and Zimon looked away from the flat screen long enough to wink at me and blow me a kiss. I frowned at him but ceased my frowning when his eyes blazed red for a terrible second. He quietly laughed. Jeremiah continued.

"However there is another type of Witch, one who walks in darkness and feeds from fear. They can live long lives as well, as long as there is plenty of fear to feed from. And sadly, this planet has fear in abundance. Serving the dark is not without its consequences. It eventually leads to madness. Unluckily for you; Kracious is very mad indeed. The word *Warlock* is an old term, and at its root it means traitor-enemy-devil. So, I do not refer to myself as such. I am a Witch; a very old, very clever Witch." He paused, winked at me, and threw a plush pillow at Zimon. It smacked him upside the head.

"I see much," Zimon grinned in return and teased. "The Witch brags much."

"Silence, leech. Please, go shower in holy water. Rid me of your sarcasm." He looked back at me and frowned. "Dead things always irritated me."

I ignored their banter and asked what had been bubbling in my chest since entering the room. "So what do I do? How will I stay alive if some evil warlock dude is intent on killing me? I know you say I have some type of "gift," but I haven't used it since I was a small child, and can't even remember how I did it then. And what the hell? Zimon is a VAMPIRE? What is WRONG with this picture?" I had snapped and was ranting. I knew it, but couldn't stop myself. I'd had enough of this stupid talk of magic and vampires and Warlocks. I just wanted to go back home, watch Animal planet, and eat junk food until I had to be airlifted from the living room. I had so reached my limit. I answered myself.

"Everything! Everything is WRONG with this picture. And had I not witnessed that evil prick pulling a dead cat from a tiny hat yesterday, and had my ex boyfriend not blown my brains all over my desk, and had a frickin' scorpion NOT been in the bathtub while Kracious sat on the toilet watching me bathe, I would call you a lunatic and leave this place laughing." I erupted into tears and sat back down, feeling very sorry for myself and very, very confused. Jeremiah just watched me with blank eyes and Zimon narrowed his own, and spoke.

"We may have some Midol out front in the shop, you know, if *it's that time of the month.*"

My mouth dropped open and I was starting to say something that would make a sailor blush when Jeremiah spoke up.

"I told you," he spoke slowly. "I will help you. Starting tomorrow our teachings will begin. I will teach you basic protection, but controlling your gift takes many, many years to perfect. However, I will make some calls. I have many friends behind the veil, and none will be too pleased with a rouge Warlock stalking the streets. He will eventually be exterminated, and you will be free."

I sniffled and punched the couch cushion beneath me in frustration. "This isn't fair, why me? What if he never stops? What if you never find him? What if he hurts my *mom*? It doesn't take a genius to figure out that he's gonna be severely pissed off when he realizes you're trying to come to my rescue."

Jeremiah held up his hand and shut his eyes for a moment. "Worry will not help matters. Whatever will be will be. But if it's any consolation, I will have your home under watch, and your mother will be guarded as well. Do not alert her to her guards. She'll likely not be able to see them anyway, unless she has a bit of witch herself." *Oh, she's got a little witch in her,* I thought, *especially when she doesn't have her morning coffee.*

"I won't," I said softly, and was suddenly overwhelmed with gratitude. He made it all sound so simple. A feeling of safety was slowly winding around my body. I was still scared out of my freakin' mind, sure, but I thought that, with some effort, I could function normally. The guy had to be a saint to pull me into his protection. I didn't understand it, but behind all of the fear, gratitude was growing.

"I have an idea, "Zimon silkily suggested. "Why not send her mother on a small vacation? Perhaps she'll suddenly be overwhelmed with the urge to visit an aunt in another town, or better yet, another state. Grace is certainly old enough to look after herself for a few days according to human standards."

I saw Jeremiah's eyebrows shoot up and his mouth lifted in agreement. "This is the only reason I haven't shoved a crucifix down your throat, Zimon. You often have helpful suggestions."

Zimon snarled at him and threw the pillow that Jeremiah had hit him with earlier. "A pity they don't burn witches at the stake anymore," Zimon countered. "I do love a good barbecue."

CHAPTER 11

The New Shadow

Jeremiah left me with Zimon – alone – which I was pretty horrified about. But he paused long enough to squeeze my shoulder and assure me he wouldn't take long as he left to make some "calls." As he went through another door at the back of the room I didn't even notice before, I noted with vague interest that it had a keypad entry. I wondered what kind of horrors lay beyond it – dead bodies with punctures on their neck, courtesy of the vampire seated across from me; or a portal to hell itself? I shivered.

"Don't be afraid, love, I had a large lunch." Zimon cooed, sounding sophisticated and suave and very freakin' creepy. He laughed at my expression and suddenly was at my side, plopping down on the couch and causing me to bounce a little with his added weight. I hadn't even seen him rise, much less cross the room. "The insufferable witch that is currently playing your knight in shining armor would cast God knows what type of horrendous spell upon me. I do not fancy boils or rabbit ears instead of my current perfect ones." He reached up and pulled at a lobe for emphasis, though it wasn't exactly what I would call perfect, just, very, very white, and, well – normal looking.

The way they both talked made me feel as if I'd stumbled into the wrong century. I suddenly felt self conscious and clumsy with my own way of accent and grammar; then I remembered that in reality they were actually senior citizens – of course they would talk differently. They both just looked so *young*.

Zimon looked to be perhaps a couple years older than myself. He was handsome, but not shockingly so. But, still, I had learned enough to avoid his eyes. His freaky vampire lure was strong. "You humans... so fragile," he said. "You live your lives without a clue of what really goes bump in the night. I suppose you know enough already to be allowed to see beyond the Veil."

"The Veil?" I asked cautiously, wondering what the heck he was referring to. I'd heard Jeremiah mention it, but was far more interested in how the heck I was supposed to stay alive. He turned his eyes on me and they locked with mine. Too late – I knew – I could not look away. However I didn't feel entranced. It seemed I was staring into his eyes out of curiosity more than anything. He wasn't using his "gift" on me at the moment, apparently.

"The Veil is what us supernatural types call it when someone is suddenly made aware of what you're seeing now. It's the underground – the place where beings that were once thought to be fairytales are walking around in the flesh. They're all around, you know. But we work very, very hard to keep humans ignorant. Can you imagine what they would do if they knew a vampire ran Elonzo's?" He sneered. "I'm not overly fond of humans myself, unless it's dinnertime. But I *do* like you so far, Grace." He gave me a look that said he believed his swagger to be unstoppable. But I was way too curious to even roll my eyes.

"Jeremiah actually let's you eat people?" I blurted before I could stop myself.

Zimon sighed dramatically, reaching for my hand and squeezing it. I gasped at the coldness of it, but I didn't pull away. We stayed like that, his hand clasping mine, and I listened to him. "Darling, sadly, we cannot pillage and yank big busted women screaming from their beds in the middle of the night anymore. We have to... sip. We drink of them, yes, but we do not kill. And if we do, it's almost always by accident. Women are the easiest... let them get a little tipsy and these country girls will follow you anywhere, not that it's hard with our gift of compulsion anyway. You experienced that earlier, didn't you, Grace?" He lifted at brow at me and gave my hand another squeeze. "We drink only what is needed... and we don't have to feed that often; usually about once a week. Anyway, three females a week, in one night... or males, it's not that difficult. They don't remember anything unless we want them to. The worst that happens is a slight hangover – and they usually would have one with, or without a vampire bite. Jeremiah knows I don't harm my humans."

I was really freaked to be holding hands with a vampire as he told me the way he was able to drink blood from people without being noticed. I think he sensed my discomfort, but he continued to hold my hand in his surprisingly gentle, cold grip.

"I do enjoy your warmth. I miss my own at times." He said, sounding far away. I was stiff as a board, wishing to wrench my hand away, but at the same time I felt a strange connection with this weird otherworldly being. He smiled at me. "And then there are the Fae... the shape shifters.-angels – and things I cannot very well describe."

My mouth gaped open. "What? Here?"

He giggled and looked at me like I was an adorable puppy that had just done something exceptionally cute. "Yes silly, if there are vampires and witches, why not the others? They're all around you everywhere you go. The Fae especially love this place... the forest provides much cover for their gatherings," He shivered a bit. "The trolls are filthy things though. Grumpy as hell and twice as ugly." I thought I would swallow my tongue.

I felt Jeremiah before I saw him; much like a warm breeze. His scent filled the room. He smelled of earth, clean water, and something spicy and undeniably male. I breathed him in and Zimon quickly released my hand.

Jeremiah looked annoyed, "Zimon, are you wanting to give the child a nervous breakdown? One can only look so far behind the veil in one day without being overwhelmed."

"Uh," I said. "I think The Veil pretty much went up in flames, like, yesterday, or... today... or... no... wait... GOD." I rubbed my eyes and realized just how tired I was becoming and took a deep breath. I jumped a little when I felt Zimon rubbing my back in what I guess was supposed to be a reassuring gesture.

"Zimon, "Jeremiah cautioned in a slow, dangerous tone of voice.

"What, you big barbarian? Can't you see she's terrified and in need of some comfort?" Zimon hissed.

"Zimon, "I said. "I really hope this doesn't make me sound like too much of a bitch, but your undead freezing hand is doing little in the way of comforting me. Especially when I know you could totally take a chomp out of my neck if you suddenly get thirsty." Jeremiah walked around the couch and flashed Zimon a look of triumph.

Zimon hissed and removed his hand, sneering at me. "I've tried to be nice to you, little girl, but your foul human manners are grating on my nerves."

I jumped a little as I felt something rubbing against my calf through my jeans. I looked down and saw a beautiful chocolate colored cat. He was massive for a domestic cat, but lean and beautiful. "What kind is he? I haven't seen many cats that color... he's gorgeous." No one answered me but my spirits perked a bit upon seeing the feline. He gracefully wound his way around and around my leg before jumping lightly into my lap. I stroked his silken fur and marveled at the golden eyes that stared back at me. "Hi there kitty," I said. His neck was long and graceful, his legs, long, his paws, small and delicate. His ears were larger than that of a regular old domestic, making him look a little like an Egyptian sphinx without the whole bald look. I noticed the gleaming green jewel hanging from his silver collar on a tiny chain. The design reminded me of a round bird cage, with delicate little bars. The green gem inside twinkled in the light of the big screen and the glow of the lamp with the drooping white shade to my right. "So pretty," I told the cat. I wondered what breed he was and resisted the urge to cuddle him against me. I remembered Snowball lying lifeless on the pavement, and then, yowling with malice after being pulled from that stupid prison cap.

"The name is Damascus, and thank you, I agree, I am quite stunning. But please, don't fondle the collar, dear. That little trinket you see keeps me alive," the cat said.

I screamed and nearly slung the cat into the floor, but he held on to my jeans for dear life, scratching my right thigh.

"Ouch, damn, stop that! How dare you ruffle my fur like this? It'll take forever to groom it back to its glistening perfection, stupid girl!" His voice was low and carried the hint of an Irish accent. I froze in panic, and knew that my mouth had to be hanging unattractively open when I noticed Zimon rolling with laughter.

"Scaredy cat," Zimon teased, and laughed even harder.

"Damascus... leave her be. She's had a very... interesting couple of days. I told you to hang back until I explained to her about you," Jeremiah said.

"Yes, well, considering she just met the bloodsucker over there and has been killed twice by that overdressed *Chris Angel* wannabe, I wouldn't think a talking, magnificent creature such as myself would come as much of a shock. She's obviously intimidated by my beauty"

I stared with wonder as the cats mouth moved when he spoke, baring his thin needle like fangs. You know those movies with talking animals that always look totally fake when they're speaking, and it's out of sync with their body movements? This cat didn't seem fake at all. He tossed his head and narrowed his eyes at Jeremiah as he spoke, the fur on his back standing up even further.

"And you are requesting that I serve as her guardian in your steed? Forgive this horrible human expression, but, *fat chance.*" In a huff the cat turned his blazing gold eyes on me and – without another word – bounded into the floor and hopped gracefully to the low wooden coffee table that sat in the center of the room. He stretched lazily and carefully to his full length on its surface, yawning dramatically and closing his eyes. Jeremiah cleared his throat awkwardly and sat on the end of the recliners seat, his long legs making him appear as if he were squatting as his weight rocked the recliner forward.

"Grace," he said slowly. And I shivered despite my being totally freaked out. I loved the way my name sounded coming from his lips. It had a slight rumble that traveled into my brain and vibrated my senses to the core. I looked at him; appreciating that beautiful blond hair falling into his eyes. He gave me a tight little smile. "This is Damascus," he gestured to the cat who allowed his eyes to barely slit open. He appeared bored and totally disinterested, but I had a feeling the effect was intentional. He was clearly pissed. But I mean, hey, how often does the cat you're petting speak to you in proper English with a charming Irish lilt? I could deal with death and time travel more gracefully than I could deal with a talking cat.

Jeremiah went on; an almost pleading tone in his voice. "Since he clearly isn't in the mood to talk now, I'll tell you a little more about him. With his permission, of course." He looked down at Damascus, the cat slowly lifting his head in a weirdly human fashion. He turned to look at Jeremiah, snorted, then resumed his relaxed pose. "I'll take that as a yes," Jeremiah said. I noticed he didn't chastise Damascus like he did Zimon. He was being cautious. "Damascus is a witch. He was in human form merely ten years ago; until he took a fancy to a very powerful Fae warrior's daughter in France. Whenever the warrior caught Damascus and Lelia embracing and, – ahem – other things, he was enraged. He then brought him before the Fae council – and though the warrior wanted his head – he gave in to his daughters pleading and asked the council for a lighter penalty. Female Fae are forbidden to consort with men outside of their kind, be they Witch, or human. With Fae men, it is frowned upon, but generally overlooked. Of course, they have their rouges that will go against the grain, but being the daughter of a Fae warrior, the crime could not go without punishment. Damascus's punishment was," He gestured to the cat, and I could hear the feline softly growl, "to be exiled to the body in which you see him in now for one hundred years, which was actually a light sentence for the Fae. He was lucky to be allowed to retain his powers. The tiny gem you see inside of the trinket on his collar allows him to live. It is charmed with his curse, and if he were to remove it, he would die. You see, the curse was sealed in blood. The blood of the Fae queen – and his own."

The cat lifted his head "And needless to say I haven't gotten my paws on the wench since." Zimon snickered and I felt my own mouth tug at the corners. Even Jeremiah smiled at the joke.

Jeremiah went on, "He is still very powerful, but a mite vulnerable in his current state. Many would love to imprison him because a charmed witch in a body such as his would be easy to slip through the cracks. Imagine, a witch that could show up on your enemies doorstep, purring and seemingly hungry, then as soon as he's through the door, smiting them with a spell. He could catch them completely off guard and with lowered defenses, so Damascus stays with me. He is, at times, a grumpy roommate, and he tends to hog the bed, but I tolerate him due to his excellent mousing skills." He grinned at Damascus and I heard the cat chuckle, which was really *effin* weird. I think that even a dog laughing would have been more acceptable. I wanted to cover my mouth with my hand when his eyes squeezed shut in mirth and his furry belly jiggled.

"Considering your horrible cooking, my friend, the rats are a retreat," Damascus teased. I hadn't even considered that an ageless witch would need food to survive. I figured souls would be the only thing on the menu. But of course, Jeremiah claimed to be a witch of light, but really, how often do you think of a witch scarfing down a hotdog with armor chili and mustard? It was all making my head hurt.

Jeremiah went on, "So Grace, since I can't be with you all the time without causing suspicion and drawing even more attention to you, Damascus is willing to assist you for a short period of time." The last words came out in a pleading tone. He nodded his head slightly and gave me a look that said *"Get it?"* His eyes said he would be very upset if I didn't.

I got it, but my tongue didn't seem to want to cooperate. How the heck would I be able to sneak him in without my mother knowing? I mean, witch or not, he would still shed, right? We didn't have any pets despite my mother being a dog groomer. Not that we had anything against them – I'd just never had the great desire to have something to take care of.

But, Damascus *was* beautiful, and I was certain he could turn on the charm long enough to get inside of the house; at least until Jeremiah could hopefully subliminally convince my mother to take a trip out of town. It creeped me out and made me feel guilty to think of him tweaking her brain, but it was far better than having her injured – or worse – dead. Jeremiah was right. It wasn't wise for me to be alone. And until he could teach me how to defend myself, Damascus was my best bet. I opened my mouth and looked down at my hands. My voice was shaky, and I prayed I sounded convincing.

"Damascus... I'm very sorry. I'm just really jumpy from all the crap I've been through lately. I didn't mean to offend you. I actually think you're pretty darn cool... not to mention *gorgeous*, and – and – I would love it if you would hang out with me for a few days. I'm scared of my own shadow right now, and I have no doubt that you could protect me." Sure, I was laying it on thick, but Jeremiah was throwing hints that Damascus was quite sensitive. I wondered if he'd always been this way, of if becoming a cat had made him softer. I saw his fur ripple and knew that my compliments had fed his ego enough to let me off of the hook.

"Apology accepted, Dear. And, please, accept my apologies for scratching you." I had forgotten about the scratch on my thigh but noticed it burning and rubbed the scratch through my jeans. "It was hard to avoid with you trying to send me airborne. And thank you for the compliments. I'm very much aware of my allure, even in this body, which is quite pleasing for a cat." He stood up and arched his back, stretching out his front paws and tipping his head forward in a stretch. The soft light shone on his chocolaty fur.

"I will accompany you and try to keep you from being brutally murdered." Damascus said.

"Damascus," Jeremiah warned. And I knew then that I wasn't quite forgiven.

"Oh, drat! Do you have to steal all of my fun Jeremiah?" Damascus sniffed.

I fished my cell phone from my jeans and realized the time. It was 6:45, and I needed to be at the park at 7. I had called my mom earlier and told her I would be studying with Amy until late. She didn't question me. She trusted me, and normally, it would be justified. But tonight I was going to meet the school geeks in the park even though a crazy witch was after me. Not to mention, I'd be bringing home another witch trapped in the body of a cat and masquerading him as a stray. I wiggled the cell back into my pocket and looked at Jeremiah. As I did so I tugged at the chain of the amulet, bringing it out of my shirt so I could hold it where he could see it.

"Do you want this back now that Damascus will be with me?" I asked Jeremiah.

"No, keep it. The future is uncertain and though I trust Damascus to keep you safe, it will be extra security."

"You just want her to wear it so you can spy on her. Not that I blame you. She is quite attractive," Zimon accused slyly. Jeremiah looked at him as if he could stake him on the spot.

"What?" I asked. Oh, hell no, totally creepy. So he could see whatever I was doing?

"It also let's him know what you're thinking, sweetheart," Zimon grinned.

"WHAT?" I yelled so loudly that everyone in the room – including Damascus – jumped.

Jeremiah tried to explain, "It is a link into your mind. It allows me to see through your eyes, and hear your thoughts if they're strong enough. Not all of them, but the ones that have the most affect on you. It picks up on strong emotions, like danger. Zimon exaggerates and is in a wee bit of a temper because he isn't able to seduce you at his whim."

Zimon laughed. "Oh, please... a human girl, not to mention one so young, certainly not my cup of blood." I cringed at the bad joke. I didn't like the thought of Jeremiah seeing into my head, but this was life or death. He was right – anything could happen – and I told myself my life was worth more than a few days of lost privacy.

"Damascus... umm... I'm ready if you are," I told him.

"Lead the way, human." He replied grumpily.

I looked at Jeremiah, my face still burning, "What time should I meet you tomorrow?"

"Try to stay home from your teachings tomorrow if at all possible. If you're able to do so, meet me here at noon. If not, the same time tomorrow will have to suffice. Come here with an open mind and a clear head... if you can," Jeremiah smiled – but his eyes were full of doubt.

CHAPTER 12

Tension

It wasn't until I'd walked the short distance to the park that Damascus spoke. "Where are we going?" he asked

I was trying to not move my lips much just in case someone saw me explaining myself to a cat, "To the park... I have to meet some – uh – friends from school. It's sort of important."

The cat groaned and muttered, "Jeremiah wouldn't like this." I ignored him and looked around. I spotted them at a picnic table. Brock sat on the table itself, his legs dangling off the side, his black and purple mohawk gleaming with gel in the streetlight. Both Shane and Chad sat side by side on the bench; their legs stretched out comfortably before them; their backs against the tables red wooden top.

It was 7:30 and I was late. I breathed a sigh of relief at them still being there. At least Chad wouldn't think I'd stood him up. Then I heard Damascus growl. I stopped and looked back and him as he briskly trotted to the toes of my feet and sat down, looking up at me. "It isn't safe here. We need to leave, *now*." The last word came out as a throaty snarl that took me by surprise. I stared down at him and cautiously bent to gather him in my arms so I could speak to him a little more privately

"Damascus... they're just kids from school. It's okay." I assured him.

He stretched his neck so he could rub his soft face along my jaw line as if seeking attention, but it was only so he could whisper, "Those aren't children, Grace. And you really don't want to meet them after darkness sets – especially not on a night with a moon such as this." He looked up and I followed his gaze. The moon was full and bright in a cloudless sky. The stars were just coming out; twinkling and plentiful. It got dark early this time of year, and there was nothing like a starry sky in the mountains. However cliché` it sounded; they really reminded me

of diamonds cast out on a blanket of velvet. A voice interrupted
my trail of thought and Damascus stiffened, his ears lying back
on his head.

"Pretty night, huh? You're late. Didn't think you'd show.
We've been waiting for you." It was Chad. They'd somehow
walked right up to me without me hearing them or catching
movement from the corner of my eye. Both Brock and Shane
stood slightly back on each side of him, and they each were
staring at the cat in my arms with weird expressions. If I didn't
know better, I would have said it was hunger.

"Yeah... it's beautiful. Sorry about being late... I... got held
up."

"It's okay," Chad shrugged. "Cool looking cat you have there."

"Thanks... he follows me everywhere. He's almost like a dog
in that way." I felt Damascus warningly sink his claws through
my tee-shirt to prickle my chest. I made up for the comparison,
"He's wonderful, though – smart too." His claws retracted. Chad
smiled, but it wasn't a *real* smile. It seemed forced and played
out, and I suddenly began to feel nervous. Were these kids even
more screwed up than I had first thought? I mean, I knew they
were fashion crippled and their social skills sucked, but were
they planning something terrible? I forced the thought from my
mind and smiled back at Chad. He was barely taller than me
and upon further inspection; I doubted he would have ill
intentions.

"Umm... would you guys care to walk me home? We could
chat while we walk," I suggested. Neither of them nodded – their
expressions blank. Chad's smile had vanished and was replaced
with suspicion.

"Sure," Chad agreed, his fake cheeriness was out of sync with
his body language. I turned around and began at a brisk pace,
clutching Damascus to my chest so tightly that he wiggled with
protest.

"How did you do on that big biology test?" Shane asked,
reminding me that we had third period together. It occurred to
me that our little town's streets were oddly deserted for such an
early night, the only visible life being the occasional teenager
that zoomed by with rap music blaring from their open windows.

"I think I did pretty well, how about you?" I asked politely.
But before he could answer Brock cut in quickly.

"We'd really like to know why you're currently under the protection of a witch," he said without hesitation. I stiffened and saw Chad shoot Brock a hateful look. Before I could even open my mouth to ask him how he had gotten that information, Brock was spinning me around to face him. His eyes were tight with fury, his mouth drawn up in what appeared to be rage. His grip hurt my arm.

"Brock, let her go man," Chad whispered tightly, and Shane repeated the order.

"You're hurting her, *let-her-go.*" Shane and Chad were both now pulling at Brock's wrist, but Brock held me firm. My heart sped up and I wished that I could run. What the hell was going on? I didn't try to fight him. I knew from the iron grip that it would be useless. So instead I met his eyes and lifted my chin. I wouldn't let him know how badly he was scaring me.

Brock looked frustrated and ready to break my neck at any second. *Anger management, anyone?* My panicked brain mused.

Broke spit through his clenched teeth as he spoke, and I felt little dots of spittle hit my face. "Not until she tells us what in the hell she's up to. You've seen it, you know what it is, and she sought us out for a reason. I see no reason for all of this stupid small talk. I say we get to the point right now." He had begun to shake and his features were twisting with what looked to be discomfort when a voice cut into the tense atmosphere.

"Release her now, mutt, or I'll see that you're stricken deaf and blind, and if you really piss me off, neutered as well." Damascus said crisply. Brock released my wrist like he'd suddenly been burned and looked around. My amulet grew warm.

Even in fear I was desperately trying to wipe spittle from my face and saying "Eww, *real classy*, Brock. Let me down and grow the hell up. How gross!" But he only squeezed my arm holder. Brock had begun to shake and his features were twisting with what looked to be discomfort when a voice cut into the tense atmosphere.

"Here, Fido," Damascus said calmly as stretched out of my arms, lightly dropping to the pavement.

"It's him, it's Damascus... holy sh—" Shane began

Chad cut in quickly. "Damascus, we didn't know she was under your protection. Earlier today she asked us to meet her and we agreed. Seeing the charmed amulet she wears; we wondered what she wanted with us. Overlook Brock... he's sort of tense and all, with the – you know." He let his voice trail off and Damascus sauntered over, sitting down in front of Chad.

"She isn't under my protection, pooch, she's under Jeremiah's." Damascus said, and I watched as Brock paled and the others followed his example. Shane gulped loudly but Damascus went on. "If you run home like the good little puppies you are, I'm sure your sires would inform you that the town is under watch. Grace here has captured the interest of a Warlock – and not just any Warlock – but Kracious. Jeremiah has intervened and broken the curse Kracious placed upon her, and needless to say, he's going to be a trifle irritated. Now, go home and spread the word." He padded back over to me and I slowly bent down and picked him back up. I didn't know how these guys were behind The Veil, and had decided I didn't really want to know.

"So what did you want with us, Grace? And why does the warlock want you?" Chad asked, his voice barely a whisper

I swallowed and began, "I just... thought that maybe you could help me. I know you guys like wizards and stuff like that, and I thought that maybe you would at least listen without being judgmental."

"You mean like the bitch squad?" Shane asked, sniffing what appeared to be snot back up into the long tunnels of his nostrils.

What she means is she thinks we're nerds and that we'd eat this stuff up, Shane," Chad said matter-of-factly.

"No... I don't. I just... the girls would never believe me. Not saying I believed you would, but I thought it was worth a shot. You just have no idea what I've been through lately. As far as Kracious, I'm really not sure what he wants with me."

Damascus cut in, his voice rising and irritated. "She can fill you in later, or your elders will, one of the two. The word is out, so be on the lookout. But for now, Grace is under my watch and it's time for her to go home." I was too mentally exhausted to be annoyed at a cat for having the gall to tell me what to do, so I just nodded, grateful for his fur's warmth. Then, though the night wasn't overly chilly, I shivered. I looked at each of the boys, wondering how they were involved in this mysterious hidden world I hadn't even known existed up until mere hours ago. But I decided that Damascus was right, and told myself I would try to piece everything together tomorrow. Shane and

Chad nodded in return, but Brock just stared at me with an intensity that made my skin crawl. I had thought for a moment earlier that he might hurt me and the others had too. Why?

I turned around and began walking. My mother would freak if she knew I were walking home in the dark, and I dreaded lying to her, but I had no choice in the matter. Damascus looked up into my face and then snuggled comfortably against my chest. I knew he had been a man years ago, but I still felt the urge to scratch him behind the ears like I had Snowball when he'd wandered over into our yard. He apparently didn't object to my affection and began to purr. After the episode with the geeks (as Amy liked to call them, and, shame on me, it stuck), I was grateful for the cat's presence.

CHAPTER 13

It's Getting Hairy...

After a while I turned on my street. I was mentally cheering for making it this far without any other freaky night people stalling me when I felt it. It felt like a cold fingernail had lightly scratched down my spine. The hair on the back of my neck stood up and my stomach began to churn. "Do you feel it?" I asked Damascus and I felt him nod.

"Just walk, human. Walk quickly," He ordered.

I happily obeyed but didn't take two steps before Kracious was standing in front of me. Clad in the same black outfit I'd seen him in last, he tapped his foot lightly on the pavement. His beautiful face was twisted in a sneer and his black eyes seemed to be gaping holes in the night. His arms were crossed over his chest and I noted the long, gleaming nails there, filed down to circular ends. They would have been beautiful under different circumstances, but tonight they appeared threatening. I bit my bottom lip to keep from screaming. I wasn't near any houses, but I was close enough for my mother to hear if she were outdoors, or any of our other neighbors.

"Someone's been sneaking around on me," Kracious said, his voice low and disturbingly calm. "I thought we had something special, Grace. But then you have to go and cheat. You've spoiled the game, and word is that you've had a little help from an old friend of mine." The amulet warmed up so much that my skin had begun to sweat beneath the silver. I was barely aware of Damascus's soft muttering. I backed up a step and could feel Damascus coiled like a spring; ready to jump. I prayed he wouldn't flee.

He took a step forward and we were once again where we'd been. He flicked his wrist and a long blade appeared. The handle looked as if it was carved out of ivory and the blade itself had to be at least the length of my leg. It was thin and light in appearance; looking very old school ninja and very, very deadly. He advanced and held it out to his side; head bent, raven hair falling into his face. I opened my mouth to scream but before I could, the air around me shimmered. Yes, *shimmered,* and suddenly, it was as if I were in a snow globe without the tiny flecks of white. I watched Kracious bounce off the front of the bubble as he lunged towards me, his mouth forming an *O* of surprise. He stepped back and, with a snarl, he punched the barrier. It rippled as if made of water but didn't budge as it glittered faintly.

I was frozen with fear but soon my curiosity overwhelmed my panic. I reached out – as if in a dream – and lay my hand on the silvery glittering bubble around me. It was warm to the touch and glowed white where I touched it, leaving a glowing replica of my hand on its surface when I took it away. I looked down, and noticed that we appeared to be floating, but upon stomping my foot lightly I discovered that the bubble ran beneath my feet as well. Glittery powder puffed up where I stomped, and had a very ticked off Kracious not been growling outside of the bubble shield, I would have laughed with delight.

"Jeremiah," I whispered, thinking him the creator of the shield.

Damascus sounded sincerely offended, "Wrong, human. You would do well to give me more credit with my abilities. I might hack up the occasional hairball, but I can cast a shield just as well as my golden haired friend." I didn't say anything, but I clutched him closer in appreciation.

"Move, girl," Damascus ordered sternly. And I did as I was told.

But then, a different type of growling reached my ears. I paused mid-step. Kracious certainly wasn't his chatty sarcastic self, he only smacked the shield once more before whipping his head from side to side, searching for the sound as well. Two came from my right, the other, – obviously the leader – from my left. They met in front of the bubble and snarled at the irritated warlock. I saw his eyes widen in surprise and then he spoke "Moon children, turn back, my war isn't with you."

They were beautiful, beautiful and impossibly large. There were three wolves, all the silver of moon beams, but differing in size. The only thing being completely different about the three that stood out were the glowing designs marking the front of their skulls above their yellow, luminous eyes. The largest of the three had a white, glowing, nearly full moon with at least six tiny twinkling stars glowing around it. The wolf at his right was more muscular, though shorter. His shoulders were bunched and rippling with barely contained energy – his neck, thick and wide. His moon was a crescent with three stars; two at the bottom right hand corner – and one at the top right. The smallest of the three bore the same crescent moon but only two stars; one at the top left hand corner and the other at the bottom right. He was sleek and graceful, and his fur appeared to be as soft as that of Damascus's. The leader crept forward slowly, baring his fangs and whipping his head. Saliva dripped to the ground. The others emitted low growls and seemed ready to pounce, but didn't follow his aggressive show of dominance. *God*, they were huge. A six year old could have ridden them like a pony around their lawn without any issue.

The long blade disappeared from Kracious' hand and he opened his arms as if in supplication. "As I said, moon children, I have no business with you. It's the girl I want." The leader sprang forward and snapped at Kracious' leg, tearing through the leather and snagging off a piece. The wolf stepped back and let the material slip from his glistening fangs then shook his head with obvious distaste. I heard the other two wolves' growls pick up in volume.

Kracious shook with barely contained rage, and the rational part of him died in an instant – if it was ever there at all. "Were you not in your true form, I would reduce you to yapping poodles. A word of advice; stay out of my way, or your pack will suffer at my hand." The three sprang at him as soon as the words left his mouth, but ended up clumsily plowing into one another as Kracious vanished. The larger of the three snapped at the others in agitation as they displayed their fangs to him, prancing and nervously growling at one another.

"That would be the three oafs you we just conversed with. Obviously the town dog catcher isn't doing his job," Damascus sniffed.

I had met a witch, a warlock, a vampire, and a talking cat. So why did I find it so hard to accept that the dorkiest kids at Birchhound were super huge, powerful wolves? Some part of me found it easier to accept the magical bubble of safety around me than it did the identity of the wolves. I mean, I'd once watched

Shane slam his hand in his own locker. He'd had to get stitches on three of his knuckles. So how could he be one of these frightening, graceful creatures?

When I asked Damascus about the markings on their heads he quickly explained that the marks told of their youth. When the glowing moon on their brow is full, and ten stars surround it, they are officially adult werewolves. The stars would materialize randomly, and sometimes in pairs. The frequency of their appearance all depended upon the wolves' mental, spiritual, and physical growth. After reaching adulthood, more stars would appear, but less frequently. An adult wolf would not be marked with more than one star a decade.

I knelt on the cold pavement and Damascus leapt softly from my arms; landing front of me. I let my fingers caress the shield and felt the pulsating warmth spreading into my fingers. It felt good, protective, and it soothed my frazzled nerves a little. The wolves all stopped their prancing and the largest came so close his nose bumped the shield, making it ripple. He plopped down very doggy like and cocked his head. Damascus sighed.

"What is it?" I asked.

"He rambles much." Damascus sounded tired.

I looked down at Damascus and while I watched he lifted a paw, licked it, and delicately swiped it over his right ear.

"You can hear them?" I questioned.

"Sadly, yes. Now, can we commence walking? I'm tired, and looking forward to the softness of your bed."

"What? You're not sleeping with me!" I protested. He might have appeared to be a cuddly adorable kitty, but he was a man – a man exiled for not being able to keep his hands to himself. He quickly looked over his shoulders and his ears lay back on his head. His brilliant gold eyes blazed with anger and became small slits.

"Twit, even if I had rakish intentions – which I do not – do you honestly think I could force my attentions upon you?" He muttered something about "stupid humans" and turned back to look at the wolves who sat eerily still in front of us. Damascus lifted his chin and sat straighter, and I realized how insulting I must have sounded. I reached out and stroked his soft fur.

"I'm sorry, Damascus," I said. "It's been a long day and I'm jumpy. Of course you can sleep with me, as long as you're not a pillow hog." I tried to put a smile into my voice, which, under the circumstances, took effort.

Sure, Damascus might have been a man once upon a time, and still was in a sense, but he was right. Even if he left me immobile with some awful spell, when it came down to being physically threatening, he could do no more than give me a few scratches. I technically wasn't his species anymore. He was harmless to me in that way. After all, I was under his protection. He didn't respond to my apology but I felt his muscles loosen and I reached down and absently began to scratch him behind his ear.

I heard a soft whine and looked up, meeting the glowing eyes of the leader of the small pack. I knew who it was the moment I looked at him; *really* looked at him. Some instinct I wasn't familiar with demanded I listen; and I did. I let my gut confirm my suspicion.

The stunningly beautiful animal in front of me was Chad Felix

"Chad?" I asked

He let his tongue roll out and panted, giving two stiff jerks of his massive head; nodding. I then got a good look at the other two. The sleeker of the two met my gaze with what I could almost mistake for kindness. He lay down and rested his head on his paws, facing me. Though still amazingly large – his bone structure was almost delicate. I assumed this was because of his wolfy youth. I saw only two stars and a crescent moon on his brow.

"Shane, that's you, isn't it?" I asked, and his ears perked up in confirmation.

There was no question about the identity of the remaining wolf. He stood on his four paws – which were about the size of a man's closed fist – and stared with eyes ablaze with dislike. I met his gaze steadily and didn't waver. If he was seeking to confirm his dominance by forcing me to look away, then he was in for an unpleasant surprise.

"Brock," I said curtly. "You might be all "big bad wolf" but you don't scare me. Trust me, I've seen worse than you lately."

He growled and I smiled bitterly.

I scooped Damascus into my arms – even though he protested that he wasn't a pet and warned me to ask permission next time. I nodded and walked, feeling the weird sensation of walking on what felt like air. My feet were still seemingly above ground, and if I weren't looking forward to the safely of my home so much, I might have tried to bounce on it. The wolves parted and moved out of the way. I looked back over my shoulder and saw them watching me. Chad looked tense and worried, Shane, sympathetic, and Brock, well... Brock looked like a coiled spring. I was pretty sure he'd rather eat me than protect me.

CHAPTER 14

Family Reunion

The walk down Formica Lane was brief. My house was the first on the left, and when I saw it's cheerily lit windows, I sighed in relief. My bubble of security vanished, and I frowned a little, missing its magical warmth already. I didn't have time to pout much, because something large materialized out of the shadows.

His hair was as white as snow, but not with age. His skin was pale, and his shoulders were so broad I was sure I couldn't touch both ends with outstretched arms. Like Jeremiah, he reminded me of a mountain, but he was far more chiseled. His eyes glowed a faint pink, making him look both exotic and daunting at the same time. His white hair hung in a long braid over one shoulder, woven with what looked like a strip of black leather.

His chest was bare aside from the beaded string slung across his chest. On his back he carried a golden bow and matching golden arrows. Intricate markings spanned the length of the bow, and, at the end of them, gold feathered halos sparkled with some strange magic. A loin cloth would have completed the picture, but instead, he wore faded, relaxed fit jeans. And to my amazement and amusement, his feet were clad in white clean Nikes. He should have been cold, but his sleek, pale skin wasn't responding with goose bumps like my own, although I wasn't sure my goose bumps were a product of the weather. Who the hell?

Damascus greeted the strange, ethereal man with eccentric fashion sense. "Adaman, meet Grace, and Grace, meet Adaman, one of our friendly neighborhood Fae warriors." Damascus sounded very polite. My knees shook as I looked down at Damascus, a million questions broiling in my mind. He went on.

"Oh, don't worry; your mom can't see them. Not unless they wish to be seen."

I lowered my voice to a whisper, wondering how many gorgeous Fae men were strutting about the yard. But I didn't see any more. "God, this is getting too weird. Not trying to be rude... Ad... Adam... whatever, but I'm going inside now. My brain needs a chance to process this episode of "twilight zone" starring, oh, guess who? ME. I'm tired. I'm going to bed now. I appreciate you watching over the house, you, and however many more there are so th—"

Damascus bit me hard on the tender skin between my forefinger and thumb. I hissed and made to toss him but he beat me to it, lightly jumping to the ground with his tail twitching in obvious agitation. His chocolate ears were laid back on his skull.

"Stupid girl! Do you know what you could have done!" He growled. I rubbed my bitten hand and tears of pain and exhaustion sprang to my eyes, burning, threatening to spill over. What had I done that was so wrong? Had I really been that much of a bitch? What rule had I broken now? Damascus sighed dramatically, and the pale man beside of him looked disturbingly amused – and maybe just a tad disappointed. But then he grinned at me and turned to walk away. Damascus shook his fur, and stretched, reminding me of a tired human. His voice was more level as he said "Never thank a Fae... never accept a gift from a Fae, never dance with a Fae, or eat their food. In short, treat them as if they're dynamite and make your actions around them extremely cautious.

"Why can't I thank a Fae person?" I asked.

"Because, you twit, thanking them makes you in debt to them, which then makes it possible for them to ask any favor they want of you before you're free and clear." Damascus said.

"Well," I said. "That's really effin' weird and all, so thanks Damascus, I'll remember that useful bit of knowledge. But let me tell you something. Just because you're a high and mighty witch cat doesn't mean..."

I was interrupted by the opening of my front door. Light shined on the lawn and I looked around, hoping the Fae dudes, however many there were, could really make themselves invisible. Mom would trip out if she saw men with bows slung across their backs strutting around the yard with her teenage daughter. She'd have a ton of questions, and no doubt the police would immediately be called. Yeah, that could get nasty. What could I possibly say to explain such a thing?

"Grace?" Her voice carried to me softly, and I immediately reached down to pick Damascus up. He hissed at me; no doubt wanting to bite me again. He avoided my hands and eased backwards into the shadows, his ears lying low on his head. I tried to make my voice sound pleasant.

"Hey Mom... sorry I'm home so late. I had to meet with my friends to study up on this new... umm... history thing."

"A history thing? On what?" The question was innocent enough and it should have been super easy to conjure up an easy lie, but a sudden brain fart left my mouth hanging open.

The words came without thought "You know... when they accused those women in Salem of being witches? We're all supposed to pick an unusual piece of history and write an essay on it. And I thought it would be neat to write about that."

I hoped mom couldn't hear Damascus's soft groan of displeasure at my excuse as he padded back up beside of me. I quickly picked him up and stepped out of the shadows, crossing on the fall browned grass to our front steps, preparing for a long tongue lashing for bringing home a stray cat. Instead I was floored. When my mother lay eyes on Damascus (who was suddenly rubbing his face on my chin and purring like a chainsaw), her eyes, strangely luminescent in the soft porch light, shined. A brilliant smile lit her features and suddenly Damascus was being gently picked out of my arms.

"Oh, Grace! He's perfect! Where in the world did you find a cat as beautiful as this? Does he belong to someone? Does he have a collar?" She started examining his neck and I shook my head dumbly, forgetting to shut my mouth as it hung open even wider. Damascus purred and turned his head to face me. He jerked his head impatiently as if to say *"Go on, idiot,"* which was totally lost on my mother as she cooed and spoke in high pitched appreciative gibberish to Damascus. She stroked his head and cuddled him close, laying her cheek on his velvety head.

"Umm... I don't think so mom. He was wandering around a dumpster at... Amy's. A bunch of us girls were there studying and I told her I'd take care of him until we found his owners – if he has any." I wondered where his trinket had gone, and, knowing it was what kept him alive, I surmised that it must have been some type of glamour that kept it hidden. I could feel

Damascus's eyes boring angrily into me as my mother squeezed him against her chest. No doubt if he could speak right now he'd be protesting me associating a cat as grand as he with a dumpster.

"Well," mom said, sounding positively pleased to the point of bursting. "It looks as if you're going to be rooming with us for a while, Mr. Tinkles!" I pressed my lips together hard to keep from laughing at Damascus's new name. Sure, I could tell her I'd already named him, but I was enjoying this bit of power over the bossy witch. Maybe he'd just pick her brain later and make her call him something else, but for the moment, I too, was pleased.

I knew later that something weird was going on, something really, *really* weird. My mother was in the best mood I'd seen her in for months, not that she's very often in bad moods, but that night it was like she'd drank a whole gallon jug of happy sunshine juice. She fussed over Damascus, talking to herself and reminding herself to buy some pet supplies in the morning, which is where the second mom-oddity of the night came in.

"Grace, if all goes according to plan, I'll be going to visit Heather for a few days. I'd invite you along, but I'd really like to spend some personal time with her, plus... you have school. And since it will take Damascus a while to adjust to his new home (She said "home" as if it were a permanent thing), I was hoping that maybe you could stay here and keep a watch over him? I just haven't seen her in so long and... I don't know, it's kind of strange... but tonight I started missing her very much."

It didn't go unnoticed that she'd called a cat she's christened "Mr. Tinkles" by his preferred name. I bristled.

"Oh, yeah, forgot to tell you. Mr. Tinkles is Damascus now. It just popped into my head earlier, and I thought it was such a pretty name. It's perfectly suitable for a beauty like him!"

I jerked. I knew what had happened. I looked around for Damascus but couldn't see him anywhere in the living room. If I had seen him, I would have thrown a shoe or a vase at his proud, fuzzy head. It was one thing to make suggestions inside of my mom's head (which was way freaky enough, thank you very much), but to play with her emotions; it really pissed me off. I wanted to yell at someone, anyone – but instead I stretched my face into a painfully huge smile, hoping it looked authentic. "That sounds great mom! You guys could catch up and talk things out. I think it would be good for you. And yeah, I kinda want to stay here with Damascus too. He needs me." Actually, it was reversed. Sadly, I needed him. Without him, tonight I would have been filet of Grace after Kracious had finished with his big sword. I had no way of knowing if he would have actually killed me tonight, but the anger in his face had suggested that he would have had Damascus and... err... the *moon children* hadn't been there to protect me.

Mom smiled and nodded briskly. "Then it's settled. First thing tomorrow I'm driving out." Her sister, Heather, lived in South Carolina, so mom was in for sort of a hell of a drive. The two hadn't spoken in over three years. When Grandpa had passed – devastating us all – he had left my grandma – of course – nearly everything he possessed in his will. But surprisingly, he had left a goodly sum of around 100,000 bucks to my mom, enabling her to open her dog grooming business. He had only left Aunt Heather (the most spoiled and doted on of the family), three grand. Heather had of course, took a major hissy and pretty much disowned mom. So this was totally out of character for mom to want to visit her. Mom left the room and soon I could hear her chatting excitedly to my Aunt Heather, "Yes, tomorrow... and yes... I'm excited too! We have so much to catch up on!"

What? Aunt Heather wasn't calling mom every vile name she could think of? Aunt Heather had a terrible potty mouth and used her words like a whip; lashing and leaving you speechless. I'd never liked her, *at all*, but there I sat, listening to the two giggle like schoolgirls excited over an upcoming sleepover. Had they screwed with Aunt Heather's mind too? I shook my head, refusing to think on it any longer.

Later in my room I was slipping into my nightgown when Damascus finally decided to seek me out. I squeaked and hurried into the clothing, glaring at him. His big golden eyes scanned me from head to toe "You could have..."

"What? Knocked?" Damascus snorted. "Don't worry, brat, your body, however lovely, isn't sending me into a fit of lust. I'm much more attracted to that big, fluffy bed of yours." With that, he jumped up, landing softly on the down comforter at the foot of the bed. He settled in and stretched out, looking perfectly comfortable. I was going to protest but was far too tired to do so. Instead, I paced to my window and looked out across the expanse of lawn. I cocked my head at the green glowing in the huge weeping willow outside and wasn't very surprised to see a couple Fae warriors. They looked to be sharing an apple, their backs pressed against the bark with their legs stretched out comfortably on the branches. I shook my head and made my way to bed. Damascus gave a small, very kitten-like sigh as I pulled the covers to my chin. I realized that for once today I felt safe, and now, not so totally alone after all.

That night, I visited hell. Well, okay, it wasn't hell, but it might as well have been. The first thing I noticed was the smell of decay, strong and seeming to carry bits of rot into my nose. I gagged and tried to spit, but my lips wouldn't open. So this only resulted in my gagging some more as my mouth filled with my own sour tasting saliva. It was dark, really dark, and I wondered for a moment if I had gone blind. I'd never seen darkness so deep. My lips felt... sewn shut. I tried to wiggle my way upright but immediately was greeted with red tinted pain as my head banged on something wooden. I felt my way around, trying to find an escape whenever it hit me. I was in a coffin. My scream was muffled and loud inside of my head as my lips painfully tried to open in a scream. I bucked and kicked and clawed at my lips until they throbbed. It was then that I heard that laugh, *his* laugh – cruel and distinguished – like him. Suddenly the lid was being flung open and my eyes were immediately drawn to the glowing full moon above.

"Grace! Honey! Would you stop that horrid noise you're making? It's killing me!" Kracious laughed. But his sarcasm was lost in my horror. I was down in a hole, the walls squared and earthen. I was in a grave. I rose up and grasped the side of the coffin, sobbing and trying to get out of the terrible box. But I wasn't going anywhere. Kracious brought his boot down hard on my stomach, making air push painfully against my sewn lips as it whooshed from my lungs. He squatted there, on his popped leg, putting even more weight on me as he leaned down. Tonight he was dressed in a very expensive looking black tux. A small white rose glowed bright against his breast pocket with moonlight. His hair was tied back in a sleek ponytail, leaving his beautiful features open and making his jaw line even more pronounced.

"Yes, you're right. You're dead, dead as a doornail, dead as chivalry, dead as driftwood. Dead-dead-dead-dead. And forgive me, but you smell terrible." He produced a tiny white silk hanky and pressed it over his nose. "That stink could wake the rest of them," he cocked his head, indicating the ground above us. And of course, I was in a graveyard. I was able to peer down at myself and saw that I was in a long, flowing white dress, which was beautiful and as expensive looking as the attire he wore. As if reading my thoughts, he said, "Yes, your mother went all out. That's a thousand dollar Dior dress you're wearing, sweetness. Although, I must say, you look better with it off." The hanky vanished and he wiggled his brows at me. "What you're seeing is your future, Grace. This is the future you have created by your betrayal. I must say, I've been deeply shaken by your cheating heart. *So much so that I'm going to break your pretty little neck the first time I get the chance.* Look around, Grace. See what awaits you."

He lifted his foot and I sucked in air loudly through my nose. I rose, looking about me. The dress was indeed, stunning, and the shoes? I would have leapt for joy to own a pair of those babies. But I didn't care about that just now. I couldn't appreciate the finery. Instead I looked at my skin; pasty and white. In the moonlight I looked at my wrists and found the veins there looking flat and dry. No blood, *I had no blood.* I began to claw at my mouth. I clawed until my nails broke. I clawed until bits of flesh dropped on the front of my pretty gown. I clawed until the thread that bound them broke free. And then his foot was on my chest, pushing me back, and the lid sounded a heavy thud as it closed on top of me. I pushed to no avail as I watched the pointy tips of nails being driven through. I screamed. He laughed. I screamed, and screamed, and screamed, and...

"Wake up, Grace! Wake the hell up before the Fae cavalry bursts in here and your mother breaks in behind them. Ye little fool. SHUT UP!"

I rose up, gasping, and collapsed back on my pillow in tears. Damascus gingerly padded and climbed up on my stomach, which still felt sore, as if Kracious had really had his weight on it. "It was him, Damascus. It wasn't just a dream. I still... hurt." I pressed my fingertips to my throbbing lips and sobbed some more; pressing the pillow to my face to keep my mother from hearing. My voice was muffled as I explained briefly about my dream to Damascus. "He said it was a vision of my future... I was in a casket... and I couldn't scream... because my lips were sewn shut and..." I couldn't finish.

Damascus sighed and surprised me by softly walking over to lie down beside of my head. "Sleep now, girl, you'll have no more dreams this night." The gentleness in his voice made me cry harder. I reached my arm up and gently scooted him close, burying my face into the fur of his side. He didn't resist, and I felt him relax while I greedily took comfort in his softness. I heard him chanting softly and all of the sudden, relaxing warmth filled my bones. I didn't remember drifting off – I only remembered a feeling of peace, and a sense of beautiful, dreamless black.

CHAPTER 15

Handle with Care

I woke not by my own choice; but by a small hand shaking my forearm. I let out a shriek and in turn caused the shaker to shriek.

"Geez, *mom,*" I grumbled as I looked at the alarm clock. 4:00 AM, what the hell?

"Sorry honey," my mother whispered, almost as if we weren't the only ones in the house and whispering was necessary. Then I felt something warm against my shoulder and realized we *weren't* the only two in the house.

She went on, "I'm leaving out for Heathers... I know it's early, but I wanted to make good time. I stopped by Rickey's and bought some groceries and some stuff for our new family member." I could hear the smile in her voice. And, geez, she'd already been shopping? Rickey's was a twenty-four hour super center type grocer which was pretty much the center of the town. Everyone shopped there. The convenience of shopping for groceries and camping gear in the same place was just all too convenient to pass up.

"Mom," I asked groggily, "Did you get any sleep?"

"A couple hours," she whispered. "But I feel so rested! Like I have slept eight hours instead of two," She laughed.

I rolled my eyes and was thankful that she couldn't see them clearly in the dark. Mom kissed my forehead and tucked my covers back in around me, telling me there was cereal in the cabinet and assuring me over and over that I could call if I needed anything. I knew she'd call me a bazillion times before she got home. She's just like that. Being extremely nice this particular morning she set my alarm clock for 6:30 and told me not to be late for school.

"Mom?" I stopped her before she quietly shut the door. "What is today?"

"Friday, hon. Now, go back to sleep so you aren't tired in your classes. And be sure to scratch Damascus behind the ears every day for me. Ok?"

"Okay," I said. "Love you."

After about an hour had passed without any success in going back to sleep, I got up and walked over to the side of the bed where Damascus lay. "Damascus... hey," I shook him gently. Suddenly I felt the pressure of five razor sharp nails on the top of my hand.

"Do-not.-touch-the-merchandise-twit," he growled.

That's when I'd had just about enough.

"I was just going to *inform* thee, O' high and mighty Garfield that I couldn't sleep. I plan on going downstairs, eating Doritos for breakfast, and watching the Discovery channel which might just be showing some of your bigger cousins. Stop talking to me like I'm an infant! Stop biting me, and stop clawing me! The next time you do I'm going to clobber you with your brand spankin' new litter box, do you understand me, hairball? Show me some respect! I've been through enough without your smartass pushing me around!" Weak morning light seeped through my dark black velvet drapes, and I saw his eyes narrow.

Oh crap.

Suddenly my legs felt really warm, like, cozy, wrapped-in-your-favorite-blanket-warm. I looked down and almost screamed when I realized what Damascus had done. There, on my legs, my formerly *smooth* legs, was thick black hair, long and kinky, and reminding me of the legs of a snuffleupagus. "What have you done? Take it back!" I stomped at him. To my horror the hair on my legs lifted with the air as it was pushed upwards by my stomps, wafting in the wind, mocking me. "Ooh!" I growled through gritted teeth. Damascus gave a dry laugh and sat up, licking one paw delicately and slowly swishing his sleek tail back and forth.

"You have my permission to go downstairs and eat Doritos. By all means, eat until you get cellulite. I don't *care*. But do not wake me unless you're in some type of dire need," he said matter-of-factly. "And do not shake me; that's just *rude*."

I was getting close to a rant that would never stop. "I'm stressed, I can't sleep, and I am in some DIRE need of some comfort food. Keep in mind that I don't know all the rules, and I don't really know *you*. So maybe you should cut me a little slack and stop acting like you have rabies!" I screamed at him. I stomped off, refusing to beg for him to make vanish the lawn on my legs. Razors were invented for a reason, I told myself. I was already spinning with my sudden knowledge of the world behind the Veil, top that with guilt for planning on misleading my mother, and your result will be a crappy morning, with, or without the luxurious hair on my legs. My mother assumed I would be going to school today. Thanks to her weird – dazed – sudden travel urge, it wouldn't be hard to pull off missing my classes. I was *so* not in the mood to deal with Amy, biology, or the weird *'Moon Children,'* as Kracious had called them.

Once in the kitchen I went straight to the cabinet that usually held cereal. I figured cereal wouldn't make me quite as plump as Doritos. Obviously, Damascus had touched a sore spot in my psyche. While trying to decide between the two boxes of cereal I held in each hand, I heard a soft laugh.

"I would choose the Fruity pebbles," said a velvety, husky female voice. I dropped both boxes on the counter; thankful the flaps on top were shut, and spun to look at the intruder. I was stunned, not only by the fact that my intruder was female, but also by her flawless beauty. Her hair, black as night, shimmered in the yellow kitchen light. I took note of the small, glittering crystals that were somehow clasped into her hair. Tiny, and delicate, she couldn't have stood more than five feet tall. Her full lips twitched into a smile at the sight of my shock. Intelligent sky blue eyes met my own, unwavering. And even though I was totally, seriously freaked out, I envied her creamy skin and flawless bone structure. Her dress, forest green and knee length almost seemed to be made of leaves. It made a swishing sound as she began to walk forward.

I finally found my voice.

"Stop it right there, girlfriend, or I'm gonna grab the biggest skillet I can find and cause some damage. Who are you? And what are you doing in my house?" I interrogated. She laughed, and I almost hated her for how it only increased her almost obscene beauty, which I didn't think was possible until that moment.

"Oh, darling, there's no need for that. Jeremiah (she said the name with obvious affection) thought you might feel a bit more at ease if you had a female around. I don't know if you've noticed – but you're right in the middle of a testosterone power plant." I squinted at her, somehow trusting the words she'd spoken. And of course I'd noticed the fact that I had nothing but males around me. It was like I'd died and gone to what I'm pretty sure would be my friend Amy's version of heaven, without the dying and creepers chasing me, of course.

"Are you one of the... Fae people? Like the guys outside?" I asked.

She laughed again, "Yes, and no. We are both gifted in weaving elemental magic, but we're different in some ways. I am what the humans refer to as a *Nymph* – a Wood Nymph – to be exact. These woods here are... extraordinary for someone such as myself. You see... I am sort of bound to this land, and these woods... we are a part of one another." She smiled and continued, "We are also far easier to love than the haughty Fae." She flipped one side of her gleaming locks over one shoulder for emphasis and gave me a meaningful look as she struck a pose with one small boned hand on her softly curving hip. Her eyes left mine and rested on the poor Aloe Vera plant my mother insisted on keeping around for its soothing properties for burns. But the thing was dying; its tips were black from having pieces snapped off occasionally. Mom has a flair for burning herself every time she cooks. So the poor plant had suffered.

"I am Esalore, by the way," She placed her hand on her chest, and I watched in fascination as she touched the plant and its black edges healed. It grew plump and larger instantly, its edges spilling onto the kitchen counter.

"There, my lovely," she purred to the Aloe Vera.

Ok, freaky, creepy, and totally effin nuts. Then I did something that surprised even me. I turned around, put the Cheerio's back in the cabinet, and found a bowl to eat my fruity pebbles in. I poured the milk, grabbed a spoon, and took a large, chunky bite, and briskly trotted purposefully past Esalore, pointedly ignoring her. "Well. That's just wonderful. By all means, make yourself at *home,*" I said the last word with venom as I threw it over my shoulder. It was only then that I remembered the abomination growing on my legs, but when I looked down, it was gone. I suppose Damascus figured I had suffered enough. I knew Esawhore, or whoever the hell she was, had probably seen them, and my face reddened with mortification

Her sweet laughter followed me into the living room and the air around me shimmered with what looked like bits of sparkly dandelion fluff. The soft scent of fresh earth and honeysuckle filled the room. Even though I was currently having a morning meltdown, I couldn't help but breathe deeply after I swallowed the cold, sweet lump of my cereal with a very unladylike gulp.

"You won't even know I'm here. I am to watch for intruders and alert the Fae if any problems arise," Her voice followed me. I didn't have to look back to know that she wasn't there.

For all I knew, Miss mythological America was floating above me turning mid air kart wheels. I put forth a giant effort not to give a crap. I was in information overload and needed this small break. There was nothing interesting on television. I allowed some meaningless talk show to rot my brain for the next hour. Damascus bounded into the overstuffed chair in my living room almost as soon as it was over. He made a big show of ignoring me. The day passed at a snails pace. I kept glancing at the clock, waiting for noon. Around eleven or so I could hear Damascus and Esalore conversing softly in the kitchen. Every now and then her laughter would ring out, clear and sweet. No doubt Damascus was laying on the charm thick. I rolled my eyes and was extremely thankful when it was time to seek out Jeremiah. Restlessness had overtaken me, and I had to do *something* to burn off my weird extra energy. I was prepared to walk the few blocks to Elonzo's when a sleek black car with tinted windows pulled to a stop in front of my house.

Damascus trotted beside of me, "Silly girl, do you think I would be foolish enough to allow us to walk these dangerous streets again?"

I shrugged and hesitantly opened the back door. The driver looked to be about fifty and was dressed as casual as myself in my blue hoodie and jeans. He gave me a quick glance; and I gaped when he turned back around. The man looked human, dressed human, but his eyes were anything but human. They formed viper like slits and were a startling shade of light purple.

Damascus leapt lightly from the back to the front seat, taking the passenger side. The man nodded to him in greeting and I heard Damascus give him a polite "Goo' day" in his faint Irish lilt. The ride was unremarkable and Jeremiah seemed genuinely pleased to see me, ignoring Damascus's complaining at having to endure what he called my *"horrible mannerisms."*

Curled up on the couch in the dim back room, I even managed to smile at Zimon who sat at the other end. He flashed me a rakish grin, his sharpened incisors visible. I suppressed a shiver and listened to Jeremiah as he took his place in the recliner across from me. I told what my mom had told me about my childhood, and his eyes never left mine.

He cleared his throat. "Well, according to what your mother has told you, I was correct in assuming that you have a bit of magic in your veins. Any clue whom it might have come from?" I told him about my father, and how I'd never met him. He shrugged. "It doesn't matter where it came from, anyway. What really matters now is that you learn how to use it. You'll need some form of personal protection from Kracious."

"Okay," I said. "So it's gonna be all like, Harry Potter, wizard apprentice stuff?" This earned me a blank look from Jeremiah.

Zimon spoke up. "Jeremiah, you should really read more, and watch more television. It's a popular book series as well as a major motion picture." He snorted and Jeremiah just shook his head.

"No, this will be nothing like... uh... that. I'm just going to teach you how to shield yourself. The rest is far too complicated to learn in the short time we have. Not to mention, we don't even know the extent of your powers. They could have been weakened over the years considering you haven't used them. It could take a while to build your strength. Come now; let us take a short drive."

We left in the same car and Jeremiah chatted easily with the driver. I heard him refer to him as "Noman"; a private chaffer. *Um, wow*, I thought. I sat in the back seat alone, fidgeting with my thumbs. We drove for maybe ten minutes until we were pretty much in the middle of nowhere. I had lived here all of my life, and found it remarkable that I didn't know the place had even existed before. When we pulled to a stop, the driver rushed from the driver's seat to sprint around and open my door. I thanked him awkwardly – not used to such fancy treatment – and gawked around me. We were surrounded by beautiful mountains without even a power line in sight. The increasingly chilly weather was turning the leaves of the massive oaks and maples to bright oranges and yellows. The wind would blow in great bursts, only to weaken and caress my skin almost shyly. The evergreens stood out, stretching out their massive arms as if to taunt the chilly air with their unchanged beauty. Storm clouds rolled, but the few patches of sky I could see were a bright, vivid blue. I breathed in deep and savored the scent of the rain in the fertile air and felt a little calmer. But I didn't have time for a retreat. I needed to learn how to defend myself, and as silly as it sounded; with magic.

A few leaves blew around me and were swept away in a mini cyclone. I focused on them, thinking I very much felt like one of the quickly crumbling leaves; safe in my perch, above danger, only to be forced into a change that left me flailing around without direction.

"It's beautiful here," I said softly.

I felt his presence before I saw him step to take his place at my side. "Yes," Jeremiah agreed. "These woods run deep and have yet to be touched by your machines that dig into the earth for its coal and strip away its trees." I knew what he was taking about. Coal mining kept the lights on — but it was tragic to watch as the mountains were decimated. I'd seen every day pretty much from infancy how a great mountain would suddenly turn bare and flat. But, still, it wasn't a perfect world. Not everything was in perfect balance. I tried to stay away from the whole coal debate. I wasn't really on either side of the spectrum. People in this area get really riled about that type of thing. One thing about a small town; piss one person off, at least fifty more will place you on their crap list, too.

I looked over at him and again marveled at his beauty. The increasingly strong wind swept his hair back from his face, leaving the white scar visible that ran down his cheek. I had the sudden urge to kiss that scar — to sink into his muscled arms and comfort him — not that he needed comfort. He was so solid, and strong, it was hard to imagine him in any type of distress. I almost wished he'd show a sign of weakness, so I could console him. The ridiculousness of the idea struck me. How stupid! Wishing for someone to get upset so I could have the chance to make them feel better. I shook off my thoughts and tried to put on my game face on. I couldn't waste time with my *"Oh muh gawd you're so hot,"* moon eyed, jaw drop that I took up so easily around him.

Suddenly my stomach was in knots with nervousness. Here I was, laying the foundation for what could very well be my salvation in my battle with evil — and all I could think about was how beautiful Jeremiah looked with the wind in his hair. I realized suddenly that a little of what I felt was more than superficial attraction, and my breathing sped up in fear of what that might mean. He whipped his head in my direction and met my eyes. The look on his face was unreadable, but I saw his jaw clench. I felt the amulet growing warm on my chest and gasped. What was going on?

"Grace... " He began, and his voice took on a husky quality. He lifted his strong, squared hand and I noticed that it held a faint tremble. And for a moment – just for a moment – I hoped he might raise that hand to my neck and pull face towards his. But instead he reached for my hand, and in turn, took the other. He *visibly* shook himself and I had the sudden urge to rip the amulet from my neck and toss it to the wind. I so didn't want him to get a read on my feelings, but I feared he already had.

His tone turned serious, "Listen to me, and listen very carefully, all right?"

I nodded.

"I know it may be difficult; but I need you to relax as much as possible. So sit down, and try your best to clear your mind. Breathe in, and release your air slowly when you begin. Then, Grace, I want you to imagine that the wind – powerful with the approach of the storm – is blowing out the many thoughts in your head. Imagine it picking up your negative feelings and tossing them up, up, and away."

I did as he said, and hesitantly sat down on the leaf riddled earth. I crossed my legs Indian style and closing my eyes. I smelled the wind – tasted the electricity in the air – and I tried to imagine it entering my nose. I imagined that with each exhale, the negative energy and the scared, confused thoughts left and were carried away. After maybe a minute or so of this I could feel my body relaxing, and my thoughts felt clean, pure.

His voice cut in, soft, and coaxing me into an even more relaxed state.

"Everything you see here, the trees, the earth, and the wind you feel – down to the water in the streams – holds energy. And if you listen... and feel... the mother earth will allow you to take some of that energy, and by doing so, the earth is not damaged; it is given to you willingly. So stand, and imagine a pulsating power is beneath your feet. Imagine the life within the trees and the grass beneath you is vibrating with a white light. Then imagine that the light is entering you, through your feet, your hands, and your third eye. Take that energy; for it is a gift. It is yours, but only to do good with."

I did what he said and almost gasped when I could actually *feel* the earth pulsing beneath me. The air warmed, and I could feel energy; snapping, bright, and energizing – swirling around me. I opened my mind, and my body, and willed the power to enter me. And whenever it did – Oh God, whenever it did, I'd never felt such joy. I'd never felt such power and peace. I would have fallen with the perfection of it all but suddenly, I felt as electric as the wind around me. I felt like the sun, the moon, and the stars. I was large and impossibly infinite. I felt like I could fly. With the power of nature rushing through my veins, I listened, I waited, and I wanted more.

"Now Grace," he sounded on the verge of bursting with excitement. His tone seemed maybe even a little disbelieving. I wondered what he was thinking. "Imagine that the power you've drawn from the earth is expanding; until it is outside of you. Imagine that it's creating a shield of warm light, unbreakable, and protective." I did as he said and immediately felt the power expand until the air around my body hummed with energy.

"Grace!" He almost shouted, "Open your eyes. Open your eyes and look upon what you've wielded!"

I did, and my mouth dropped open. I tried to hold on to the energy – afraid it would blip out – but what I saw stayed visible. The same protective bubble Damascus has encased us in the night of Kracious' attempted attack, now glowed around me. And this time, I couldn't contain myself, I jumped up and down with delight. The most amazing thing was that – without realizing it – I had expanded the bubble to surround not only myself, but Jeremiah as well.

His eyes were alight with excitement when he spoke, "Never before have I saw one shield so quickly! I can feel your power, Grace, and it is very strong. This power the earth has lent must be returned – but while you hold it – you can make it do your bidding. Imagine what you want, Grace. Imagine anything, and watch it be. Materialize it. Everything is energy, *everything* – and anything you want can be built with it."

I tried to do as I was told and imagined, of all things; the little pink treasure chest I'd had as a child. Inside were such treasures as plastic *Barbie* crowns and plastic beaded bracelets.

I pictured it manifesting at my feet. Years ago it had broken, and I'd thrown it away. But since then, I wished I had held on to that precious relic of my childhood. And let me tell you, I almost peed myself when it appeared at my feet.

Jeremiah whooped with joy, "That's it! That's it, Grace! You're using power to manifest. Anything that can be produced by man – you can manifest. Think of it, all man made items have their roots in the earth. And right down to the power of the lightening itself, if you're wise and patient, you can call at will." I grinned and noticed how tears were suddenly filling my eyes. Such a gift; such a wonderful, super cool gift I had been given. I didn't know why, and I knew I'd pick this gift to pieces later, but at that moment I was so happy that the snot and tears didn't kill my smile. I'd had so much stress and horrible near-death situations over the past few days. This amazing power I'd just began to tap into was like a rainbow right after a storm; a promise from my creator that I was not alone.

Jeremiah went on, his eyes alight with feverish delight, "There are certain spells you can use also. The words can be different, but the instructions must be clear. Different spells require different things, from a drop of your blood to a ritual with herbs and oils. But that's for later, right now, we focus on protection. And as of right now, I am very pleased. Your shield still holds strong!" He swatted at it for emphasis and its glittery surface crackled with what seemed to be static of some kind. I reached out and touched it, loving the warmth that spread through my fingers. I also loved what Jeremiah had said. My heart sped up at what it might mean. '*But that's for later*,' which meant that I would be spending more time with him.

At his instruction, I imagined the power seeping back into my body and leaving through my feet, hands, and third eye – back into the elements which had loaned it to me. I also willing the box away; sparing an affectionate smile. I knew it wasn't the same one – just a replica, so it didn't pain me too badly to let it go. We walked back to the car I almost jumped out of my skin with delicious shock as Jeremiah slid his arm around my shoulders. He smiled at me, and I tried to tell myself it wasn't the type of smile reserved for a baby sister that had just made an *A* on her report card type of smile. His arm, warm around me, couldn't have felt more perfect.

CHAPTER 16

Bliss

We made it back to Elonzo's and were greeted by the ever perfect Esalore just inside the door. But Esalore didn't seem quite as beautifully calm and collected as she had this morning. She walked up to Jeremiah and, to my horror, wrapped her slender arms about his neck and kissed his cheek with a slowness that pinched my soul. What the hell? Was I *jealous?* Jeremiah would never want me, and the feelings were extremely annoying. She pulled back.

"Dear one, it has been much too long," she cooed.

"I agree," he rumbled, his eyes sparkling with obvious affection. "Thank you for the favor you've done me this day, I'm sorry I could not ask you in person, but I have been terribly busy ensuring Grace's safety."

She pouted "Yes, that girl seems to be quite popular lately with the lesser beings (she said "that girl" as if describing some bug she'd squashed with her tiny green slippered feet) but I am not here to chide you for your absence. I am here to pass along the message that the Fae have asked me to give you. The Collector is about, and word is that Kracious summoned him from the underworld for one purpose – and one purpose only."

I saw the color drain from his face, "It can't be," he whispered.

She went on, "It is rumored that Kracious has declared war on the local Fae. I do not think he would have done such a thing if it were only here and the collector; even though they are both powerful. We are all in agreement that he must be summoning more demons for his army." She sniffed, expertly causing her full lower lip to tremble. And Jeremiah was an idiot, because he reached out to squeeze her arm, comforting her. Her voice choked as she went on. "I am so afraid, my love. Mere minutes ago our dear friend Amelio was found smoldering by one of the local sprites... he is... gone from this world. The Collector then tortured another warrior for information, but the warrior would not crack. He is in near death – and seems to be suffering from some type of poison – he is the Queen's only son, Jeremiah." A shudder went through her that actually looked real, and I saw Jeremiah's eyes widen.

Esalore went on. "Even so, the collector allowed him to live so that he could pass along a message... to the girl – though Famorsh grows weak and raves with hallucinations. The Queen is said to be very angry." Esalore removed her hands from about Jeremiah's neck and walked over to me, her hips swaying, and stopped dead in front of me, "The Collector said to tell you that he's going to fetch your soul, by whatever means necessary." I gawked. What the friggin hell did that mean? And who was "The Collector?" Once again I felt as if I was slipping down the rabbit hole and my eyes actually began to twitch.

She turned like a runway model on her heel, her green dress softly swishing. "I must go, Jeremiah. An entire night and afternoon without the forest; and I am weakened. Do not hesitate to call me if you need any other assistance, be your summons related to this particular crisis, or a personal crisis..." She winked at him and I had the sudden urge to rip out her perfect hair. She slinked away and in mid stride vanished into thin air. I didn't even have time to gawk before I was suddenly being propelled to the back room of Elonzo's by Jeremiah's massive hand on the small of my back. "You're not going home tonight," he told me.

"But... but... my mother, she'll be calling, she'll worry," I protested. I knew that as soon as my mother realized I was absent and that Amy had no idea of my whereabouts, it would be very likely the local National Guard would be on a manhunt in about an hour. I shivered at the thought. My mother was a sight to be reckoned with. Once she got fired up – people would do her bidding just to escape her loud logic. I wouldn't be surprised if she'd convince the local sheriff to do a home search of every house in the county – with – or without a warrant. She was just that convincing.

Damascus was stretched out on the back of the plush couch, and Zimon sat in his usual place on the far left side of it. Jeremiah left me standing in the middle of the floor and quickly walked over to Damascus, saying a few quick words.

"Very well," I heard Damascus murmur lazily. He stretched then quickly bounded off to the front of the building through the beaded curtains.

Jeremiah walked back to face me, his eyes burning into my own. His jaw was clenched and I took notice of how his fists clenched sporadically. "It is taken care of; your mother will be called."

"What? You can't call her! She'll totally freak and think someone's holding me hostage or something. Are you insane? What are you going to tell her?"

"Damascus... will be calling your mother." He cocked his head, listening for something, and I felt the hair on the back of my neck stand up.

A voice – *my* voice – was coming from the front room. The creepy me was freakishly cheerful sounding, and assured my mother that she would be studying late at the library tonight on the Salem witch hunts. The voice also claimed to be staying with Amy at the moment. I shivered when I also heard a perfectly pitched Amy giggle and yell in the background, "Hi Misses Sprinter! Hope you're having fun with your sis. Grace and I are totally gonna OD on extra buttery popcorn tonight. I heart yooou!"

"Holy sh—" I began, but again he shut me off.

"You're to stay here. I will be back in a couple of hours." He actually *pushed* me down beside of Zimon on the couch with his hands on my shoulders. He pointed his finger at me as if I were a toddler he had to remind to behave in his absence. I shot him a glare.

"But, who is *The Collector*? Just answer me that. I need to know what's going on. And what did she say about the Fae and about a death? Please, Jeremiah, clear the confusion for me?" I was pleading with my eyes for a shred of information; otherwise I thought I'd die of morbid curiosity.

"Zimon," Jeremiah said. "Tell Grace all she needs to know about the day's happenings. And give her some history on the collector." Zimon nodded and for once wasn't being his sarcastic, grinning self.

Damascus trotted back into the room and jumped up into the recliner Jeremiah had occupied the few times I'd seen him. "Yer mum says she's having a great time and that she's currently playing a game of poker with her sister. She was laughing, and informed me that she's already won fifty bucks. Personally, I believe she was blitzed off of her arse. But she seemed genuinely pleased that you wouldn't be alone and would be staying with Amy tonight." I took note of how Damascus's faint Irish accent was stronger when he was being a total turd.

I gaped at him. Mom, blitzed? Drinking? Eww, I so did not want to think of my mother doing anything recreational. I shook my head and again thought of how totally out of character such a thing was for her. She seemed so... mellow. It was creepy. Apparently she and Aunt Heather were now bosom buddies and having the time of their lives. I was betting they'd even painted each other's toe nails. I was glad she was having fun – I mean – she never had time to just let go. But I would much rather think of she and Aunt Heather playing a dry game of bingo and making handmade quilts than taking shots. I groaned. Damascus had imitated my voice perfectly, and his impression of Amy was even creepier; considering I knew he hadn't even met her before. I asked him how he'd managed it but he only sighed and told me I didn't need to know *everything*. I then threw a whole string of rushed questions at Zimon – knowing my voice was high and sounding a wee bit hysterical – until he held up his hand. I bit my tongue and waited.

"There have been many different... beings patrolling the area around your home, so we're all quite shocked at how The Collector managed to kill one of the Fae and torture another. You see, the Fae may be quite pretty in appearance; but war is in their blood. Only something as clever as the collector could manage to break through the protection spell placed around your home *and* manage to kill one Fae and injure another without alerting everyone around the perimeter. The Collector is very ancient. He may have watched as the dinosaurs roamed the earth, or perhaps it was later. We have no way of knowing his true age or origin. He is typically in sprit form, and harmless, trapped in the underworld – only able to torment those below, that have been condemned. Once summoned with a *very* complicated ritual – which no one has done in generations – he can choose the body of anyone with a dark spot on their soul, which – realistically speaking – is anyone beyond infancy. I have personally never crossed his path, nor do I wish to. Even in my long life I have never heard of anyone successfully summoning him. According to legend; any attempt only results in madness and death on the person foolish enough to attempt it. He's become sort of a... " – he searched for the word and laughed humorlessly – "*fairytale*. He's one of the most favored demons in the underworld, and quite easily one of the most deadly. We don't know very much about him; just that fables that claim he wields a great whip and has the ability to rip a soul from its very body. Actually, I had thought him a myth until now."

Not. Good.

My stomach dropped. Yes, I was scared, yes, I pretty much knew it was very likely that some demonic spirit was going to come and gobble up my soul and take it down to hell. But what bothered me most of all – what made my nausea roll – was just sinking in. One Fae had died for me, and another had endured torture for my sake without even knowing me. Tears filled my eyes and shameful color crept into my cheeks. I hadn't shown any appreciation to the beings I'd watched wondering the lawn the previous night, scanning the road and the hillside, sometimes laughing with one another, eating, and talking. They had seemed so... human. And if not for their otherworldly beauty; could have passed for such. Guilt crept inside, black and slinking, and dug its jagged nails into my heart. A very special man had died, and it was all because of me. Now the Fae could possibly be sucked into a war. And it was all my fault. Why the risks for one girl?

That Fae and the other, were tortured? Oh... oh... " I sniffled and murmured softly, "This is all my fault." I wondered if he'd had a lover... a wife... children, and my stomach felt sick. I didn't resist at all when Zimon placed his cold hand over mine.

"There... there... it isn't your fault. You didn't ask for Kracious' attention." Zimon soothed.

"No," I said, my voice rising in pitch with the suppressed years I refused to let spill. "But I'm also not comfortable with people I don't even know dying for me. It's ridiculous. I'm just a seventeen year old kid that – truth be told – has been sort of spoiled. No one should have to die in my name. No one owes me anything. I'm thankful... very thankful... but I'm not worth it."

Zimon cocked his head and I turned my own, meeting his eyes.

"I tend to disagree. Jeremiah does not offer his help to just any damsel in distress. He's taking a giant risk with aiding you – he's creating enemies – fast. Those on the other side of the Veil don't take too kindly to humans learning our secrets, but then again, you're not the typical human with your unique history. And besides, Jeremiah and the Fae know that if it hadn't have been you Kracious took a fancy to; it would have been someone else. Or he would have just caused calamity in general. He's gone quite mad, and they see him as a threat. They knew he was in town before he even cursed you, and were already planning action against him." I allowed this to sink it but it didn't kill the guilt. I wondered how Zimon knew about my childhood – my differences from everyone else – but didn't ask how he knew. I'd gotten pretty used to these folks knowing just about everything about everyone.

Zimon went on, "The warrior died in honor. He was placed there for one reason – and one reason only – to protect you. The Fae queen herself sent the Fae after Jeremiah asked her to. Everyone knows that if Kracious wants you so badly, there's something unique about you. Our little part of the world is peaceful, and Kracious' games are forbidden."

He met my eyes again, and I found myself staring into his own. Such a beautiful, odd hue of green, I thought. And were they glowing? Or was it a trick of the light? Damascus bounded off the recliner – apparently oblivious to the awkward moment going on in front of him – and headed for the front room. Around that time the doorbell rang, and I heard Damascus thanking someone for the safe delivery of his pizza. How the hell did he do that? It hurt my brain to think about it.

"Couldn't he have just made a pizza appear in the drop of a hat?

Zimon sighed, "Overuse of power is never a good thing. Even a stupid cat knows that." I thought that was equally stupid considering Damascus had likely used his power to disguise himself. No delivery guy would leave without screaming if a talking cat opened the door and paid for pizza.

He kept looking at the beaded curtain and pretty soon we could hear Damascus chewing somewhat loudly behind it. I tried to imagine if I'd ever seen a cat eat with its mouth closed, and decided I hadn't, which explained his loud munching. He may have been a powerful witch, but he was still in a feline body. A sudden wave of sympathy washed over me. Strange, how the weirdest things like Damascus chewing very kitty-like could bring out my softer side.

I heard Zimon's breathing turn labored and I looked him square in the eye. His lips parted and I watched with awe and fear as his incisors grew long and sharp. I began to cringe away, but I continued to stare – not because I was powerless to his allure – it was because he was trying to relay my fear through the eye contact. But suddenly, he was squeezing my knuckles so hard together that I cried out. Before I could even finish my cry – he was on me – and a bright explosion of pain erupted on my neck where he'd sank in his teeth. After a moment, the pain turned into bliss. The feeling that came over me was so perfect that it shouldn't have existed.

I wanted more. I begged silently for him not to stop and I pleaded in my head for all that he could give. I could have died and would have been content if the fire of my life was extinguished with his bite. I could think of no better way to die. I felt him hesitate for a moment and I groaned in frustration. If he stopped, I would scream. I would scream until my throat closed and I breathed no more. I told myself that he couldn't possibly be so cruel as to deny me. And then in a blur, he pressed me closer and bit in, deep.

"Zimon, you leech! Release her, this instant. Jeremiah will pierce you through your heart with a pool stick if he learns of this. Good God man! Are ye daft?" Damascus's accent was suddenly so thick that I couldn't understand it, but Zimon apparently did because when he heard Damascus he released me, and allowed me to tumble unceremoniously to the couch like a ragdoll. I lay limp on my back, lacking the strength to even open my eyes.

My blood was on fire, but my body wasn't under my control. Numbness replaced the feeling of mobility and I found that I couldn't even swallow. It was like being paralyzed all over again. But even the sting of the deadly scorpion hadn't numbed me this quickly. I wanted to get up – to run – somewhere, anywhere; now that whatever high I had been swept away on rudely dumped me back to earth. Suddenly I was disgusted with myself. How in the hell was I supposed to protect myself from one of the most badass demons in Hell when I couldn't even defend myself against Zimon's suggestive, paralytic stare?

I could see Zimon place his elbows on his knees and cradle his head in both hands. "I-I don't know what came over me. You see... I haven't fed in... going on three weeks now. One moment she was just like any other human, tasty smelling, sure, but not irresistible. But then... she met my eyes and wouldn't stop looking. I was weak. I would have stopped immediately with a taste but it was almost as if *she* were the vampire and *I* was the one in thrall. Her blood was like pure power crackling... and in my head – I could hear her coaxing me on. While I drank, if she would have told me to slit my own throat – I would have gone to find the sharpest knife in the drawer." He laughed, but the laugh was tired and, if I didn't know better; scared.

"I should turn you into a bat, you chode!" Damascus slicked his ears back and I could feel him pounce and land neatly behind my head. "Why have you gone so long without feeding? Are you mad?"

"I've been lazy... " He sounded miserable. I could feel him get up and heard his soft footfalls on the carpeted floor as he left the room.

"Couch potato!" Damascus growled. "All he does is watch HBO and then he wonders why he's slowly starving himself You'd think after watching *"True blood"* every week he'd have learned something."

Was I dying? And *what?* Zimon watched *"True Blood?"* Even under those circumstances, I would have laughed if I could have. That was so *lame.*

"There, there, chit," the insult was there but I also detected something like a fatherly concern in his voice. He rubbed his velvety head against my cheek and snuggled in beside of my head; leaning close to my ear he spoke a stream of words;

With love and light, I release your chains.
I cleanse the tainted blood from your veins.
With each beat of your labored heart,
Love and light fills thee, and weakness departs.

I might as well have been doused in ice water. My heart sped up and my blood thundered inside of my head. I rose with a gasp, almost sending Zimon into the floor.

"Watch it!" He cautioned, but I could hear the pleasure in his voice at the effectiveness of his words. Tears sprang to my eyes and I picked Damascus up, squeezing him and kissing the top of his furry head. "Easy girl, you're squeezing too hard! I am not a stuffed animal!" But he didn't scratch or bite me, so I continued hugging him, although a little more gently.

"Thank you Damascus! I couldn't move. Zimon just, well, he mauled me! What if he would have killed me? Why is everyone *always* trying to kill me?" I said in a defeated, small voice.

Damascus sighed.

"He wasn't trying to kill you. He was simply starving – but he'd rather watch bad reality TV and horrid movies than go out and stalk prey. He an idiot– yes, but a killer he is not. The poor parasite is beating himself up with guilt as we speak. He also believes this will be his last day on earth if Jeremiah learns that he, ahem, sampled you." Damascus said.

I raised my lip in disgust. It was almost like being compared to a glass of wine in a tasting contest. The feeling of the bite had been *amazing*. Zimon was right about one thing; I had urged him on in my head. I hadn't realized he could hear me until he'd mentioned it, but I was just as much at fault. Had I struggled, I think he would have released me. But the bliss of a vampire's bite, I had learned, was impossible to deny. Then I remembered his voice, how guilty and defeated he'd sounded, and I sat Damascus gently back down on the couch.

"I'm gonna go... um... talk to him," I said. Damascus nodded and sprawled back out, completely unfazed by the entire episode.

I found Zimon behind the counter; his head hung low, his handsome face contorted in what looked like disgust. I came up behind him and gingerly placed my hand on his shoulder. Normally I would have called him names that would have even made my Aunt Heather blush, but I was feeling particularly sentimental today. I decided that must be from lack of sleep, but nonetheless, I went on.

"Hey, it's okay. I understand you have... needs... and yeah... I did... umm... ask you not to stop, in my *head*. And I don't know how you heard that but yeah... I certainly didn't say no. It just... well... you know the effects." I cleared my throat, feeling awkward and wanting to put this behind us as soon as possible.

He raised his head and turned to look at me, his face blank. "Jeremiah is going to have my head on a stick and my testicles in a jar. I'm sorry, Grace. I would never hurt you. I *like* you. I just grow careless with age. I tire of luring women out of bars. You see... I'm enjoying the longevity of my life... but I also tire of it. I-I am not always pleased with what I am, and so I find myself staying home instead of hunting. Today I didn't realize how famished I was until it was too late. My apologies, my lady, please forgive me."

The sincerity in his voice broke my heart, considering it was coming from one of the biggest rakes of the century. "Hey, it's okay. Just... maybe you should... umm... " I couldn't finish. I *so* did not want to encourage him to go bite some hooker in a bar or some drunkard on the corner.

"I will, as soon as night falls. I refuse to leave you until Jeremiah returns – even though I haven't done a great job of protecting you so far." He laughed bitterly and his eyes found my neck again. My eyes must have bulged from my head because he held up his hands "No... no... it's just, you have a wound. And if you'll let me, I can fix it." I wasn't very convinced but when I reached up to my neck and felt those two nasty puncture marks; they felt incredibly gross and my hand came away bloody. I met his eyes – searching for assurance – and found his expression to be clear and his hands steady as they reached for my head. He tilted my head to the side and my breathing sped up. I was scared, disgusted, and almost, *almost* wishing I could feel the awesome rush I'd felt earlier again. But Zimon – true to his word – only made contact with his tongue. He slowly ran it over the marks left on my neck, released me quickly, then walked away.

I reached up – amazed at the smoothness of what was just moments ago a nasty wound.

I went back into the den in the back and watched in silence with Damascus and Zimon, of all things, *"The Wizard of Oz."* The silence was only broken when the *"Wicked witch of the West"* made her appearance. Damascus thought she was hilarious. I napped on and off, and so did my companions, *especially* Zimon – whom I figured had been making an effort to stay awake so long. He slept unmoving, his head lolling on the couch. He slept – well – like the dead. Despite him biting me earlier, I didn't feel afraid. Had I not been so exhausted, I likely would have slept with one eye open. I drifted, and didn't complain when Damascus sought out the warmth of my lap. I stroked him idly and smiled when I heard him purr, and eventually fell into an exhausted sleep.

CHAPTER 17

The Collector

The one who had summoned him stood giggling and dancing from one long leg to the other, clapping his hands like an overly excited child. The Collector was immediately annoyed. Did this ridiculously garbed black haired creature believe he was in control of such a powerful being? Did he think he could order the most preferred weapon in Underworld to do his bidding? He; the shepherd of souls in the underworld, would have curled his lips in disgust were he not just a wispy vapor above the earth. Below... he had a much more suitable form. As large as an elephant, with massive horns jutting forth from his grotesque crimson head – he was magnificent and terrible to behold. The Collector took pleasure in flaying the flesh from those that dared to so much as lift their heads from their constant submissive bow. With the crack of his whip from one of his large, muscular arms, he devoured their terror and pain with complete pleasure. He did not know love. He did not know mercy. He was an intelligent machine. He only felt lust and the darkness that fed his cruelty.

Once he had walked the earth in all of his obscene glory. He had roamed with one purpose – to find those behind "The Veil" that evaded death through magic. Whenever a veiled one became too powerful – too experienced at evading death – The Dark One would send The Collector to speed up their biological clock.

Now – few knew of him. The world was wrapped in a protective bubble; a bubble that deemed beings such as himself legends and fairytales. So The Collector was hidden away. Most creatures now chose to evade human contact. It was much the same in Underworld – until a mortal died, anyway. So after being taken from the earth, he became the foreman – he became the punishment.

He gnashed four rows of razor teeth upon his charges putty skills, relishing their boiling blood with a tongue that was small in comparison. He would occasionally slip a soul for his own personal pleasure; sucking what little remained of the doomed spirit's essence into his great maw and sending them to that place that was even more terrible than hell; the dark.

He would roar with an almost sensual pleasure as he struck their backs. The crack of his whip kept them busy for all eternity. Pointless work; shoveling – carrying large boulders upon their backs – crawling upon their hands and knees through fire with menial tasks. Those sent to the eternal fires were his favorites. Their faces would melt away as the skin crisped and charred. Their very eyes would burst in their sockets from the intense heat, but they did not perish. The whip did not only torture – it healed. Whenever one of the damned became unrecognizable – with nothing but gushing veins for limbs and a tough piece of leather for a tongue – the Collector would restore them and let their torture begin anew. Such cruelty was reserved for the lowest of life forms. Those that neither walked in the light, nor danced in the darkness, were merely forced into an eternity of brutal labor. But the trash of the earth – the thieves and murderers and the evil ones – the men with qualities The Collector would admire in different circumstances – were banished by the light into the insufferable heat of The Underworld.

His existence was bliss. He never tired in his true form. He did not sleep. He did not converse with the others in power. He answered only to the Dark One – and when it came to the Collector – The Dark one was never disappointed.

But someone had summoned him. The man with laughing eyes offered a brilliant smile. The Collector wished for his strong arms back – which were roughly the width of a minivan – so he could whip this weakling into submission. But then the dark haired man began to chant. He then slashed his own pale hand with a small dagger and tossed his blood upon the earth. The Collector jerked as if he had been struck in bodily form. The man's grin vanished; replaced by a grim line. As he chanted with a language both ancient and familiar to The Collector, a dark, slithering glob of power began to grow in the air above the man's head. It shrieked and writhed as it slinked down onto the man's arms; covering them first. It then began to grow; covering the man's body. The black haired man suddenly went still, and then his muscles began to jerk. A muffled moan could be heard above the shrieking and wet sounds, and The Collector wondered if this it were a moan of pleasure, or pain. He concluded that it was both. Whenever the man was completely covered with the slick mass of darkness, it sank into his skin; vanishing. The man gave one final jerk as he tossed his beautiful black hair back in what looked like almost erotic bliss.

The Collector was enthralled, and more than a little curious. He watched the man as he slashed his palm again and resumed his chanting. He then walked over to the quivering mist that floated in strange anticipation, and more than a little rage. The Collector struggled, and then ceased in awe as he pondered the feeling. He couldn't remember ever being afraid.

The man's eyes had taken on a sickly green glow, and as he moved, the already seasonally browned glass burned beneath his thick leather boots. He opened his palm, and with a glance, the blood began to pour from the almost fully healed wound he'd made only moments prior. Did he not understand the consequences of summoning The Collector? Why didn't he fall to his knees and beg for mercy?

The dark haired man flicked his wrist and circled The Collector, trapping his wispy form within a wall of fire. The power! The darkness! Such exquisite evil within such a ridiculous body, he thought. The Collector mentally quivered with delight. The Dark one had neglected him as of late – not bestowing compliments and praise as he once had. But until now The Collector had never felt bored or underappreciated.

The man spoke, and as he did he stretched out his hand, palm up. A green light pulsed, and as if spawned from an unseen projector, images came into focus. A girl with an unruly mane of red hair lay curled up on a couch. Her brow was relaxed, her breathing; deep and peaceful. The stink of light and purity had somehow invaded his senses, which The Collector didn't even know he possessed in this form. He wanted to break her. He wanted to taste the terror of a clean soul. It had been ages! Thousands of years spent consuming the souls of the tainted ones now seemed dull and unsatisfying. And then he felt it – more power – but of a different sort. The girl was a white witch! If The Collector would have had a mouth, he would have drooled.

"You are bound to me now... Great One... and you will do as I say." The man spoke.

The Collector laughed without sound, but his incredulity must have made it past the barriers of his form, because the man frowned; just a flicker of emotion that was quickly replaced by a mocking grin.

And then suddenly he was suspended in The Dark. The place where he'd send the unfortunate ones that dared to defy him. Far from heaven – and a step down from hell – he teetered on the brink of blind darkness.

And then he was back – terrified and delighted. He wanted a body, no, he needed a body – so he could bow and touch the man's boots – so he could grovel and roll in the stink of his madness and power. The Collector, for the first time in years, felt excitement.

The man's black eyes closed and the corner of his mouth twitched. "Kill anyone that resists you. Leave no one in the light that stands in your path intact. Find... her. But do not consume... Dear One... bring her to me. Her comrades are yours."

The Collector drifted in search of his new form. It didn't take long to find a nervous junkie pacing an alley that stood smacking a vein in his arm with two fingers as he clenched a needle in between his teeth.

CHAPTER 18

Purple Flowers

I dreamed I was in a field of flowers. Purple petals floated gently on the breeze, – too gently in fact – none of them ever touched the ground. They lazily passed by my head; suspended, defying gravity. The flowers themselves sort of reminded me of carnations. They stood erect and fat with peals, but when I looked, each flower bowed its beautiful head and they swayed in perfect sync with one another.

I smiled, thinking that Kracious would never construct such a beautiful world void of death and darkness. It was all mine, and I intended on enjoying the brief respite. Flowers – a sea of them – for as far as the eye could see. I lifted my face to the cloudless, purple sky and sighed with relief.

I plopped down among the flowers, pleased to feel that they didn't have thorns of any kind. I picked one; inhaling the scent. It was instant delight. They smelled just like grape Kool-aid.

The slow most of dreams cradled me. I recognized the slightly drugged feeling, the unreality, the peace. Yes, it was all mine.

I was idly picking petals and watching them float upwards instead of flitting to the ground when doubt intervened. The fog of dreamy unreality vanished. Someone might as well have drop a big yellow school bus with 'WRONG' written on the side in bold font. My vision became clearer – the soft, cotton like bed of alien flowers hardened and pressed cold and ridged into my back. The stems suddenly felt pricked my skin and became hard as stone. I raised up; whimpering as I did so. I picked a prickly stemmed flower from my hair and sucked my thumb when blood beaded from the small puncture. It didn't feel like a dream anymore. The floating petals fell as one and I jerked as red lightning split the sky.

And then I saw it.

Something was cutting through the flowers at an insanely fast pace.

Something was coming for me.

I stood up shakily, ignoring the pricks and scratches from the flowers. I ran. This wasn't my dream anymore. Kracious had trespassed.

I ran.

It was only then that I realized I was barefoot. I was also wearing the white Dior dress I'd been buried in merely a nightmare ago. High pitched squeals sliced the air around me and vibrated my eardrums.

I didn't make it far. I barreled straight into what felt like concrete. Panting; I lifted my face and stared into the black eyes I'd come to know so well. He reached up; tugging at something clasped in my hair. A few tresses fell into my eyes and he quickly – almost lovingly – brushed them away.

"I've missed you, Grace," he croaked, almost brokenly.

I heard wheezing squeals and what sounded like snapping jaws. A wet, clicking sound – somehow the most disturbing sound of all – carried to me. Something yelped in pain. There was more than one. I didn't dare turn around.

I remained silent. I didn't move. I just stood there pressed against him, mesmerized by his blank, black eyes. If anyone else could have glimpsed us, they might have thought us lovers. His eye twitched. His beautiful lips remained carefully relaxed.

"I wasn't going to play anymore... Grace. You're special... very special. You see, I had to lure out your talents. Sometimes we can only bloom to our full potential through suffering. Do not be fooled... Jeremiah is the one who wants to trap you. He's being a greedy boy... a very greedy boy. He wants to use you, Grace. Power, he craves power. But me? I only want a pupil; a student, a partner. You could be my queen, Grace. You could become a light to the world. You and I together could do great things for humankind. Grace, I know you desire me..."

He ran his hand down the small of my back, but before he could get any further I unfroze; lifting my hand and smacking his smooth, hairless face. The sky turned black. The things behind me squealed with what sounded like glee. Kracious grinned.

"All right, you little tease. Have it your way. You want it rough? I've never been one to deny a lady."

I trembled. I knew what was coming. I didn't beg, I just took a step back and balled my hands into fists.

I wanted to know what they were, but I didn't ask. I wouldn't show him my terror. This was a power struggle, and I didn't dare show weakness.

Behind me, the squealing turned to overexcited whistles and pants. Something latched onto my calf; its teeth sinking in with minimal effort on its part, I supposed. I felt them slice through my flesh as if it were hot butter. The skin pulled away.

But I never looked down.

I squeezed my eyes shut. I didn't want to see the nightmares that proceeded to eat me alive – even as I screamed.

CHAPTER 19

Blood and Magic

Someone was shaking me – hard. How long had I been asleep? I didn't even have time to rejoice that my horrible dream death wasn't real. "Wake up!" It was Jeremiah. "Wake up! We must leave, NOW!" he bellowed. I jumped and wiped at my eyes, trying to focus on Jeremiah in the light of the flat screen. His eyes were large and wild, and various weapons were attached to what seemed every part of his body. I heard a loud rummaging and looked towards the hidden room just in time to see Zimon emerging with lots of dangerous looking weapons strapped to his body in much the same fashion. Damascus stood beside of Zimon, his golden eyes wide and alert. The lights suddenly burned to life without anyone flicking a switch as far as I could see – or even clapping.

"He's coming," Jeremiah said, his formerly full moth now pressed into a white, grim line.

"What?" I asked. My sluggish brain didn't want to cooperate.

"He's left a line of the *veiled ones* dead in his search... and it won't be long before he finds you. According to legend; He has a very keen sense of smell."

I shivered and tried not to paint a picture in my head of a beast sniffing and snarling, saliva dripping from its jaws. My eyed widened even more when I saw Chad, Shane and Brock walk in. Their faces were all blank, but Brock's still had the trace of a sneer when his eyes found mine. Chad quickly approached Jeremiah, talking quickly.

"Word is that he just ripped through Pablo's asking for information about you, Jeremiah. The clan has this place surrounded, and we'll try to keep you covered until you're gone. Anvil has agreed to close the portal when you go." I looked at these boys, so common looking. Shane had earbuds and an iPod clipped to his pocket, and again couldn't wrap my head around the fact that upon full moons they turned into the beautiful beasts I'd seen just last night. I noticed another man hanging back behind them; an older guy I'd seen once or twice around town doing common things like buying milk and walking his giant Saint Bernard. His hair was white, and cut in a grand-pappy flat top. He wore grey slacks and a pain blue sweatshirt, his old sneakers looked like they'd seen better days, but the intelligence I suddenly glimpsed when he met my eyes made him anything but ordinary.

"I will close the portal and shield the shop until you have taken your leave. But the girl... she's never traveled before... are you sure, Jeremiah?" The older man asked, clearly skeptical about the whole thing.

Jeremiah looked at him squarely and assured him, "I will hold her tightly, she will not be lost or be harmed. She is under my protection, and nothing will touch her."

I had no earthly clue what was happening. All I knew was that they'd said the words *"portal"* and *"traveling"* and it was totally tripping me out. I stood up and swayed – but the fog of sleep quickly left me as fear sparked adrenaline pumped through my veins at break neck speed.

I grabbed Jeremiah's arm and knocked the unruly, bed head hair from my face with an impatient swipe of my hand. "Where are we going?" I asked.

He didn't meet my eyes as he said, "To a friend of mine's home in – well – it wouldn't be wise to mention the name within hearing of the others, just in case Kracious or The Collector decides to force information from them in some way." He let his voice trail off and I understood. He didn't want to run the risk of the others being tortured and telling our enemies our location if they happened to fall into unfriendly hands. I didn't push him further; for once. I just nodded and tried my best to prepare myself for whatever was to come. My guts were twisting and I held back a bark of anger when I saw Esalore slink past the beaded curtain and enter from the front of the shop.

"I'm here, darling," She smiled. "It is high time we get to spend some time together... though I wish it could be under different circumstances.

I bit my tongue and resisted the urge to whine at Jeremiah like a child and beg him not to let Esalore come along. Tonight she was dressed in a white gown of some kind of gauzy stuff. To

my horror, about eighty percent of it was see through. She
appeared to have on a cotton tube top and... yes... white panties
that I could see clearly when the light hit her just right. I might
as well have turned visibly green with the jealousy I felt as
Jeremiah – even in his distress – turned to look her up and down
appreciatively.

The wolf boys all walked from the room through the beaded
curtain. As they passed Esalore she gave them a seductive smile
and waved. I heard Brock say something like "Ooh cha cha cha,"
as they disappeared. I heard the normally painfully shy Shane
whistle low through his teeth. Damascus quickly followed them,
saying something to the boys that sounded quite a bit like
orders. I looked at Jeremiah "Isn't Damascus coming?" And was
shocked at how desperately I wanted him to say yes. Imagining
leaving without the witch cat that I had reluctantly grown so
fond of basically overnight filled me with dread. I needed him
around to pet and snuggle when I was scared or hopeless. Even
though he wasn't *really* a cat, he made me feel better in that way
only pets can.

Jeremiah left and went towards the back of the room and –
in front of a bare wall – began speaking softly and quickly. A
pinpoint of blue-white light began to manifest and grow. He had
totally ignored my question about Damascus. As if sensing my
worry; Zimon approached covered in gear and answered for him.

"Yes, Damascus is just giving orders to the Moon children
and Fae stationed outside of the shop."

I heard the front door shut as Zimon finished speaking and –
from the audible lack of footfalls – knew that Damascus was
coming back into the den. What happened next passed in a blur.
I heard snarling and screams outside and strange whirring
noises that my spinning brain assumed was arrows flying.
Damascus, who had just passed beneath the curtain, seemed to
flip in midair to face the direction of the commotion just as a
large, black whip parted the colored beads. Fire lit the length of
what could have been leather, flickering and sparking and it cut
through the air. It struck Damascus, and a huge chunk of his
chocolate fur flew. He was hurled backwards and landed, limp
and bleeding at my feet. I screamed and immediately dropped to
my knees, reaching for him. "Hurry, Jeremiah!" The older man I
had just discovered was a witch shouted. I glanced over and saw

that Jeremiah hadn't even looked back; his focus was on the swirling light that was growing inside by the second.

The thing that came through the doors had surely walked straight out of my most disturbing nightmares. He wore a long tattered brown trench coat that buttoned to his neck, with large brown boots. The boots were caked in some odd, blackish, oozing substance. A matching brown hat that reminded me of something some '50s detective would have worn was tilted – almost rakishly – to one side. He had obviously been sort of human once, but whatever poor soul he had possessed looked anything but human now. His cheeks were split – ragged and fleshy – from each corner of his mouth almost to his ears. His gums were fully visible, and the bones of his cheeks and jaws we're morbidly bright against the red of his muscles and joints. It reminded me of the Joker's smile from *Batman,* that is, if he'd had a run in with Hannibal Lector. The monstrosity seemed to be grinning. The eyes were black holes with red in the center; blazing, hideously alert. The hands were black and visibly charred; but the creature seemed unfazed by the unholy flames that wrapped around his hand as he wielded his whip. His head jerked, and his focus was fully on me. The smell of his – death and burning flesh – hit me like a gust of wind. I gagged through the tears that had begun to leak from my eyes.

It spoke in a low grumble that sounded full of phlegm and malice, "He has summoned me from below, and I walk the earth once more! I have come to do *his* bidding. You, child, shall know the sting of death. Repent to whatever God you worship if you wish, but it matters naught, for your soul is mine."

I trembled. This was it. This was the big finale in my crazy, weird, horrible, funny, amazing struggle. I was going to die, and not only that, but this big ugly gangster from hell was going to have my soul.

But then Zimon was running towards the monster and something whistled above my head, and – as if in slow motion – I watched a red ruby bejeweled dagger come to rest with a sickening pop in the creature's right eye. It bellowed and sank to its knees, pulling at the protruding object and opening its gaping maw into an impossibly low scream. Black smoke suddenly surrounded him, and then it was if he'd never been there at all.

"Now, Jeremiah! Now, so I can close the portal and leave with my head upon my shoulders!" The old man shouted; his face turning red with obvious frustration. I saw Esalore running towards the portal – poised at its entrance – a combination of horror and defiance on her beautiful face. She laid her hand on Jeremiah's back, and I watched as the light pulsed with energy and whatever the hell else portals pulse with.

In a daze I saw that the light had grown tall and narrow. It had become a door of light. Zimon smacked me firmly on the back and shouted, "Move Grace, move!" And as if waking from a dream; I snapped into action. I scooped the pitiful cat at my feet into my arms and cradled him like an infant, burying my face against his own as I ran. Zimon had grabbed the material on the shoulder of my hoodie and was pulling me along. As I reached the portal, Jeremiah opened his arms wide. Without hesitation, I turned my back against his chest and allowed him to wrap his arms around me. I didn't know if Damascus was aware, I didn't even know if Damascus was alive, but I clutched him to me as if he were a lifeline. I wept openly, not caring that snot was grossly running into my open, gasping mouth. Jeremiah walked me forwards, his arms tight around my midsection – so tight I could barely breathe. Zimon cut around us and ran through, his form disappearing in a burst of light, and at almost in the same moment, Jeremiah was pushing us in. I dared a glance behind me and noticed Esalore's arms were around Jeremiah's neck. Her eyes squinted as she pressed herself against him.

And then light was exploding all around me, and I was falling, falling, yet flying. The only thing I was aware of beyond the bloody Witch I clutched in my arms which – when it came right down to it, was just a vulnerable animal, magical or not was Jeremiah's heart slamming against my back.

"Hang on!" he shouted, his lips against my ear.

About the Author

Selina Fugate, full time mother by day and avid writer by night, spent most of her childhood devising clever ways to sneak into her mother's mystery novel stash. Board books just didn't compare to dime store tales of deception and romance.

She resides in the mountains of Hazard, Kentucky with her two toddlers. When she's not searching for sprites in flower buds, she reads any fiction she can get her hands on. Obsessed with black boots and driven by a fierce love of peanut butter, she plans on leaving her mark in the world of Young Adult fiction.

Also from BlackWyrm...

by Brad Parnell

Young Robert journeys to another world. There he comes of age amid a feuding government, grotesque monsters, an ancient ancestor ...and a couple of teenaged girls. With the help of a young wolf named Louie, Robert is introduced to the wonders and perils of a strange land called Gwerinatha.
[Allegoric Celtic Fantasy, ages 12+]

by Ian Harac

One FBI agent
One geekette
One dead munchkin
Parallel worlds galore
An interdimensional conspiracy.
When Matt Anders stumbles across the body of a dead munchkin in a suspect's apartment, a conspiracy begins to unravel that leads him on a reality-jumping adventure to the magical Land of Oz... and beyond!
[Snarky SciFi Thriller, ages 14+]

STRANDS OF DEATH

by Dirk Vandereyken

In a small village, a necromancer stands trial. At the center of the universe, the Spider that wove All watches intently. Webs are spun in the courtroom, of magic, of lies, and of scandal. The mage Baour argues that he supercedes not only man's laws, but god's! What he truly wants may only be uncovered through testimony. As strange magics meet strange deaths, can the reality behind it be unmasked? And should it? [Fantasy Legal Thriller, ages 18+]

by Jason Walters

At the edge of the known world, two desperate armies struggle for the right to siege a city that has never been taken. Terrible magics are unleashed and the fate of empires hangs in the balance. Highdome and his crew of cutthroats, monsters, and mutants don't care. They just want to stay alive. But when sorcery backfires and the fury of the Vast White desert is unleashed, the men and women of the Red Regiment must look inside of themselves to find the strength to survive.
[Dark Military Fantasy, ages 14+]

Albrim's Curse

by Trevis Powell

All young Albrim wanted to be was a master bowman like his father. Then a savage attack on his home cost him his family, his arm, and his humanity – all at once! Crippled and contaminated by the Curse, his beloved Gran leaves him in the care of Mute, a giant warrior dedicated to protect-ing humanity from the depre-dations of the Quarg. Albrim does what he can to assist his master and redeem himself. But can a werewolf ever really recapture his humanity?

[Epic Werewolf Fantasy, ages 14+]

Gran's Secret

by Trevis Powell

Her son is dead; her grandson Cursed. Gran has to send him into hiding to protect him, and to protect others from him. But there are those who hunt Weres to use for their own evil purposes, and they are backed by the resources of kingdoms.

When these hunters begin snooping around Gran's village, there's nothing a sweet old lady can do to protect her grandson from such people, is there?

Apparently, you don't know Gran.

[Epic Werewolf Fantasy, ages 14+]

CPSIA information can be obtained at www.ICGtesting.com
Printed in the USA
LVOW030401051111

253375LV00004B/13/P

9 781613 181089